BLUE OF THE WORLD

STORIES

DOUGLAS W. MILLIKEN

TAILWINDS PRESS

The following stories originally appeared, in slightly different forms, in the following publications: "Adventure Stories for Men & Boys" in the *Adirondack Review*; "After the Intromit" and "Pillars" in *Slice*; "A Thirteenth Apostle's Star" in *Camera Obscura*; "Blue of the World" in *Glimmer Train*; "Boys' Life / Rough Frontier" in the *Lascaux Review*. "Butterscotch" in the *Maine Review*; "Gold & Rust" in *Per Contra*; "Fraises des Bois" (as "Horse Story") in *Midwest Prairie Review*; "Hyacinth & Waxwing" in the *Stoneslide Corrective*; "Pretty" in the *Lindenwood Review*; "Saltwater Baldwin" in the *Cortland Review*; "Saw-Whet" in the Wooden Leg Press chapbook *One Thousand Owls Behind Your Chest*; "Skidder & Draw" in *Portland Monthly*. "A Fluent Blue" was originally composed as part of a multimedia collaboration with the metal smith Cat Bates.

Tailwinds Press
P.O. Box 2283, Radio City Station
New York, NY 10101-2283
www.tailwindspress.com

Published in the United States of America
ISBN: 978-1-7328480-0-9
1st ed. 2019

CONTENTS

*For Barbara and Donna, whose endings
were the beginning.*

Now something is becoming clear to her that she has failed to consider all this time: If no one knows she exists any longer, who will know there is a world when she is no longer there?

— Jenny Erpenbeck, *Visitation* (trans. by Susan Bernofsky)

BLUE OF THE WORLD

PILLARS

It was an intuitive animal-prayer when he was younger, how he'd stand outside for hours in the summertime and gaze up through the night's silence at the stars. No telescope or even binoculars. Just naked eyes. He'd stand in the patchy grass as far from his dad's trailer as he dared and stare up until his neck hurt and even then, keep staring. So many bright tiny errors in a perfect black screen, but he knew: the blackness was the error, the distance between each light. Yet still, the lights could all be seen. It filled him with hope that there might be something better out there.

Hope means a lot.

But now he's older and lives in a city where the nights have been replaced by an orange haze soft against the black. Sometimes a moon. More often: high airplanes, passing. Where could they all be going? Late when his wife lies safely asleep, he sits in the pale glow of his computer's screen, clicking through the space program's archive of deep-space photography. All the universe catalogued by wide-array telescopes. The collision of galaxies. Columns of dust stretching through centuries. Stars birthing or fading away. Light visible only to mechanical eyes. He stares at the Crab Nebula and the Tadpole Galaxy and the Pillars of Creation, and feels the deep icicle of loneliness pierce clear through him, all the way through and then deeper still. Almost to the end. Then a little more. The loneliness never passes out the other side.

It's not just the magnitude that breaks him. It's something closer. Like missing someone to whom you still have something important to tell. Someone you love who doesn't know. You want so bad to tell them. But they aren't ever coming back. They'll never know. So much beauty, so vast and far away. They don't even know what they are.

SALTWATER BALDWIN

Ethan's message was waiting for me when I got home late that night. I'd been flying for the company—had spent all morning en route to Boston, where I lingered just long enough to trade bags with a man I met in the terminal before turning around and boarding the same exact plane to come home—so I was already feeling justified in playing hooky for a day. The voice on my machine gave me the excuse I needed. A favor asked from an old friend. The little company man would have to wait. I turned out the studio lights and lay on my pallet. I fell into a dreamless sleep.

With these sorts of things, I'm guilty of too many blind spots. I don't remember when Ethan and I met. For a while it seemed we were both around the same places, in the company of the same people. Like when you pass the same person every day on your drive to work. You don't know him and he doesn't know you, but five days a week at six-fifteen, you pass along the same stretch of road. Two strangers waving hello. It wasn't until one summer a few years back, when Ethan took on a contract harvesting seaweed and asked me to help him out, that we really became friends. We spent five months in a low rowboat together, holding close to the shore and hauling great swaths of ribbony green up out of the ocean's gut. Then we'd heap it all into the bed of his pickup. It was an old Ford made sometime in the 70s that still ran like a tin-can dream. I remember, when the bed was full, how the seawater poured through the gaps and rust-holes in shining streams, splashing and clapping on the rocks underfoot. It was a music I could almost understand.

We did that together for three summers straight—just two men, silently at work—until his dad had his stroke and Ethan took over running the family orchard full-time. Then my current company found me and liked me for how little I talked. In the years since, by circumstance, Ethan and I have rarely visited or spoken. Then he called me while I raced above the earth at several thousand feet, asking for my help, and again our lives intersect.

It was almost dawn when I woke but I knew I wouldn't be sleeping any more. I lay on my pallet and watched the light-shapes cast by my window shift and change across the ceiling. Then I called out from work. I didn't even wait for the little man's response. I hung up and dialed Ethan's number.

"Samuel?" Through the phone, his voice sounded dry as an old hinge. "That you?"

I ran my tongue over my teeth. Then I swallowed. "I'm coming."

I hadn't the tools that I used to but I still had a pair of hand-pruners from Switzerland that I'd kept oiled and sharp. I supposed Ethan would have most anything else we could need. I drove out of town and for a while more under shore-side woods, then turned off where two big rocks flanked a driveway cutting through ragged coastal pines. I'd been this way before. We met in the front yard of his family's big white house and shook hands—there was the farm-stand along the driveway, all boarded up for the season, and a row of hubbard squash shining blue in the frosty grass—then we climbed into that same baby blue Ford and drove out back. He looked just as I remembered, tall and wooden and grey. His sister and someone they'd hired—a Jamaican man whose name I never learned or don't remember—followed in another vehicle. We passed through an uneven, rocky meadow of bleached seagrass, then down toward the sandy bluffs where the orchards ranged by the water.

There was a time in my life when the care and

propagation of trees was my prevailing motive and occupation. But that life was over by the time Ethan and I became friends. This wasn't my first time visiting his family's orchard but it nevertheless confounded me still that it could exist. Exist and thrive. Never before had I heard of fruit trees surviving in saltwater and sand. His family's trees were beautiful.

It was late December but felt more like April without any snow, a thin milky fog rolling in off the bay. On the other side of the inlet, dimly, I could see the town where I lived. It was just past dawn. High and full, cutting through the fog, the moon did the work of the sun.

Where I did my business for the company, there was a man who I felt was torturing me, though I understood it wasn't personal. I just had to work with him more than anyone else. I took the brunt of him. He was a short man, so maybe that had something to do with it. He'd feed me misinformation so that my work would come out all wrong. Or he'd very calmly offer me something—a binder of receipts or my own jacket or some food—then, just as calmly, would throw that something against the wall or floor. He had a doctor's notice, I guess, explaining this behavior, but mostly he was the owner's son. So whatever complaint I might file had no bearing on his continued employment. In time it came to feel as though this behavior was the sole purpose of his job. Getting paid well to make life harder for me. It didn't bother me at all, skipping out for the day.

Though I guess it isn't fair to say that the trees grow all in sand. There were deep veins of rock in the orchard as well. Mostly long granite knuckles of ledge. So for the trees, the sand was a sort of treat. We parked the trucks on a high stony slope above the orchard, then gathered our tools and headed down. Ethan and the Jamaican paired up to prune one row. I was to work with his sister.

Which, I have to admit, disappointed me. There was nothing wrong with his sister—Evelyn was her name, rosy-cheeked from chapping wind and pretty though hard and by this I mean fit, a joyful woman who'd worked this land each day of her life—but I wasn't friends with Evelyn, I was Ethan's friend. Maybe there was a motive in having us work together, I don't know. But I knew Ethan had a new son, his first, born in the summer, and in the months since learning this news, I hadn't been in contact, had not congratulated him or asked after his growing family. It made me feel like a shit for not having done these things. I hadn't thought to ask about his boy in the short ride over from the house to the shore. I'd have to wait more for another chance.

There were other trees in the orchard that weren't so

close to the water, Russets and Gravensteins and Rhode Island Greenings tumbling up the grassy slopes above us, their naked limbs making witchy shapes against the foggy sky, but the rows we pruned were those closest to the water. Evelyn used a pole saw to take out the higher boughs. I used my Swiss hand-shears on those below. It pleased me to cut through branches as big around as my wrist, but I didn't kid myself too much about it. I'd kept the tool in good shape. It was doing all the work.

In the row beside us, Ethan and the Jamaican had a similar process going on. Down the line, we thinned and shaped the trees into open rising pyramids. All our trimmings we stacked in knitted piles like beaver dams in the path between the trees. I supposed they'd dry these and use them to light fires. I felt fine out there. Evelyn would laugh each time a big branch came crashing down, like this was some playful game of sorts. I've always liked it when people take a joy in their work.

After a little while, their father came walking through the trees to join us. He didn't seem much like anyone who'd had a stroke. His hair and beard were white and he walked with a slight limp, but he otherwise moved with the speed and force of a hungry bear. He took to helping clear the trimmings for us so we could focus on our business of pruning. I don't remember anyone telling me his name.

Late in the autumn after our first summer in the shallows, Ethan's chipper busted. He called me up and I came over the next day and together, in the barn connected to his family's house, we got the machine running right. This was the first time I'd seen his place. Before we got to work fixing the chipper, he took me for a walk through the orchard. Showed me where the first trees were planted, where he and his father had extended the rows, adding varieties. His grandfather bought this land to raise his family and a few beef cattle, and only later discovered the lone apple tree growing with its roots in the salted sand. It was a Baldwin. Wine dark skin and flesh almost stony. He planted his first rows the following spring, right alongside the original. As if it would set an example. Which, in its way, it did.

"This is the tree," Ethan told me then, "that our whole farm is named after." Then with a delicacy I'd rarely seen he detached a ripe fruit from among dark green leaves and handed the apple to me. I buffed the skin on my shirt, and smelled it, and bit in. The taste of sea salt and caramel lingered on my tongue through the day.

Something easy can be more work than a difficult task you love. It's the loving it that makes it light. Our movements took on the mechanized regularity of a precise and complicated folkdance, but once when Evelyn ran her saw through the meat of a hardy branch, it was almost by accident that I caught it when it dropped. She hadn't seen that I'd moved over. She thought I was somewhere else. If I hadn't had my arm up already to shield the fog-diffused light from my eyes, the branch would have racked my skull for sure.

Evelyn got everyone's attention by gasping a little bit right then. But the danger was already averted. For one moment, I held the branch barehanded over my head like I was waving a brand or flag. Everyone was watching. Then, like a taut rope snapping, we laughed.

On paper, I am the little man's foreman. On paper, the little man is a dozen laborers. Mostly Mexicans. Men with saws and machines, sculpting the land by my instruction. But on my first day, there was no crew. Only the little man.

"Where is everyone?" I asked.

We were standing in the garage at the maintenance warehouse, between a dump truck and an articulating tractor. The little man had his hands knit behind his back. His blue eyes were fixed and hard.

"Take attendance," he said.

"What?"

He took a step forward. "Do roll call."

So I did. I read the names off a clipboard.

"Rusco."

"Here."

"Martín."

"Here."

"Escobar."

"Here."

I didn't go any further. The garage smelled like sawdust and oil. The little man, I don't think, had blinked once.

"You tell me what to do," and he took another step forward, poking at my chest with a stubby finger, "just once, and I'll kill you." Then he slapped the clipboard from my hands.

It didn't take me long after that to figure out what kind of place this was. I filed work-orders for jobs that did not exist. I wrote out payroll for men who weren't real. Some days I rearranged every tool in the warehouse. Other days, I threw everything away. Only rarely was my true use in the company employed. More often, I waited. I managed an invisible crew. Invisible forces managed me.

One time while we were out seaweeding, Ethan and I came upon this great fish lying flat on the surface of the water. I couldn't tell you what kind it was. Something with jaws like an alligator. It was two feet long or more and lay with its jaws just about unhinged with another fish caught in its mouth. The eaten fish was as big around as a softball and stuck in the other's open craw. Both fish were still alive. I remember feeling pretty amazed—what could possess something to do that, to try to swallow whole an animal nearly its same size—but Ethan just looked disgusted. All the lines in his face were drawn down.

"Greedy," was all he said. Then he whacked them both dead with his oar.

We'd been working for a few hours when the water started to change. It'd probably been changing for a while before we saw. The moon was full and the solstice was near so we knew if only by intuition that the tides would be very high, but this was different. Like each new wave came six inches farther up the shore. There was no wind or any big ships to raise a wake. All at once, the ocean wanted more. Over the rocks and into the orchard, the saltwater crept silently in.

We were already cut off from the trucks when the old man noticed the flooding. He and Evelyn took to hauling the trimmings to higher ground, I guess thinking that the cuttings would damage the trees if left to float around. Or maybe they really needed that wood. While Ethan and I located a pile of oak stakes in the upper orchard, the Jamaican waded through the encroaching tide to fetch a box of heavy twine from Ethan's truck. The water was shin-deep when he left. It was up past his knees when he came back.

It seemed like a futile measure, but who was I to say? This was their family land. We set to work pounding the stakes as deep as we could into the sand. If we hit ledge, we pulled the stake and tried again. We lashed guy lines from the stakes to the trees. If the tide came this far and stayed, it could wash out the sand, uproot the trees and carry them away. Any amount of anchor would help. This is what we wanted to believe.

But already I could see it wasn't working. The first tree Evelyn and I had pruned—the one closest to where the tide was flooding in—was already listing above the sea now at its feet. I don't think anyone else saw what was happening. They were busy. But I saw. The founder tree was being washed away.

The body responds while the brain tries to explain. It was like I was seeing something I could almost remember. Then I remembered. And then I forgot. I dropped the stake I'd been holding in my hand and raced across the sand. I'm sure I had my reasons. My footprints filled up as I ran.

Water was swirling around my knees when I reached the canting tree, its surface slithering while beneath I could feel the sand sifting like I was standing on a nest of snakes. The tree's roots were visible through the foamy wash. It was floating. I knew if we got it ashore, we could rinse its roots in freshwater and wrap them in burlap, keep the tree stored in a dark cellar until spring. Replant it on higher ground. It wouldn't be the same, but it'd be saved. I wrapped myself around its trunk and heaved and held on. I wouldn't let it go.

And further back, they were shouting. Above the sound of waves, I could hear my friends speaking my name.

"Samuel!" Ethan called, then his sister, more plaintive: "Sam!" Their arms were waving in crosses over their heads. They could see something behind me that I couldn't see. I had no idea what it could be. I didn't want to know. I fixed my feet deeper in the shifting sand and held on.

BOYS' LIFE / ROUGH FRONTIERS

I remember hearing this one story about my uncle almost dying, or anyway, maybe just wishing he was dead. He'd moved out here all the way from California, ostensibly so he could be closer to my dad and the kids but maybe also because everyone has this real romantic notion of what living in Maine is supposed to be like, all wood smoke and flannel and moose steaks sizzling on an open campfire, though regardless of his reasons, in the long haul, it clearly wasn't worth it. He barely lasted a year up here. Black flies hobbled him then the winter did him in and in between, the only work he could find was at the truckers' paradise on the north side of town where the main drag reverts into a numbered highway heading straight into whatever freezing nothing abounds above us. There was a diner and a convenience store and showers and a mechanic shop and, of course, a million gas pumps, and it was these last two things my uncle's job was all about. Pumping gas and changing filters. A bottom-rung grunt among the grease monkeys.

So what happened was, he was working the all-night shift during what anywhere else in the world would be called a blizzard, and sometime after midnight, a Canadian tanker truck comes rolling in to refill the underground diesel tanks, so my uncle has to go out there and shovel off the opening and pry up the lid and all that shit, you know, make sure the fuel goes into the ground but not a whole lot of snow with it. Given what winters were like here forty years ago, it was probably negative-thirty out, but let's be conservative and just say it was well below zero. My uncle was out there forever waiting for that tanker to drain out while the north wind cut without break across one thousand potato fields just to slice straight through his trembling marrow, and you know, I don't think he'd have been too damn surprised if the frozen casters of his nuts popped free to roll down the legs of his insulated coveralls and shatter like glass on the pavement. California can't prepare any man for this. Just the same way that this can't prepare any kind of man for California. When the tanker was finally emptied and the porthole or whatever to the tanks underground was properly sealed again, my uncle just about ran back to the mechanic shop. He was really looking forward to hunkering over that blasting oil heater inside. But it hadn't occurred to him that the shop—always kept toasty if not downright hot—would be between sixty and a hundred degrees warmer than the outside air. He walked into that wall of sweet, sweet heat, felt his stomach flop like a landed blue fin on a dock, and fainted right there in the open doorway with snow already blowing in and piling on his back.

Imagine passing out like a wilting daisy in front of all your redneck coworkers, just because you got too warm too fast. Now imagine trying to live that down. No one had told him that vulnerability is nothing we can admit to in these climes. But he'd learned. It wasn't long before my uncle was hitching a ride home to California.

But what's this got to do with you? What's this got to do with me standing here now in the frozen food aisle, comparing prices on jalapeño poppers? I drove the extra thirty miles across the border to the Grand Falls grocery store I know stays open late because I don't like shopping with anyone else around except the other weirdo late-night shoppers like me. Old ladies with carts loaded with cat food cans and lonely guys staring wonderstruck at a sale rack of Lean Cuisines. All of us winners. No need for eye contact here! There's Christmas music playing even though New Years was weeks ago and I am here now remembering my uncle's ill-fated frontier adventure but remembering too the summer you and I shared a tent on the shore of Echo Lake and mowed lawns for Dave Christmas's Lawn Care, how our boss never tired of rolling up to any job site and announcing *It's Christmas in July* although we sure did. We'd sit outside our orange nylon dome slapping at the flies in the pink break of evening, just two smelly boys squatting in our trunks and building up the courage to plunge into the icy lake water. But once we were in, it was the air that felt cold and that we needed courage to brave. We'd sometimes take turns being the fucker, pick the other one up and throw him in, and all our extra cash went to Thursday nights at the pub where the special was dollar Icehouses and twenty-five cent wings. Cold beer and hot sauce, buddy. Those were the extremes of our summer. No concerns whatsoever for college semesters past or future and not one worry that we'd grow up to be small town chemistry teachers or whatever it is you've become. I remember, there was that one day we should've skipped work altogether, should've gone to a movie or to the Aroostook Centre Mall or anyplace air conditioned, but no, we needed the money, so we shoveled mulch all day onto all the new saplings planted in the Walmart parking lot, slow-roasting in the blacktop haze like a couple of stooges, blind with sweat and woozy and sunburned even through all our SPF, and at quitting time Dave Christmas showed up with a six-pack of Heineken and the beer was so sweet and cold and wet that neither one of us could help it, we both pounded our beers with greedy lips then immediately puked from the shock, making a mess of our shoes right there in the baked August potato dust blowing in from across the fields. I remember, it was still cold coming up. Was it cold for you too? And yeah, I'm remembering how after a week of sharing a tent, that first night when it was so hot that we had no choice but to get hotter, to get delirious with heat and slaked on sweat—then afterward we opened the tent flaps wide to let the night breeze cool our salted wet skin so that we shivered and huddled back to back. I'm remembering that first time, and I'm remembering every time after that, too. How we learned to get better at this rough boys' life. Washing up in the lake with a bar of soap inside a sock. Drinking camp coffee made of lake water, too. We got good at building fires. Enough years have passed that I can now say for certain that that was the best summer of my life and I probably knew it then, too, knew that things probably weren't ever going to get a whole lot better for me, but that didn't stop me from dropping you like a bad habit once classes started up in the fall. They call that *ghosting* these days. You ghost instead of explaining why you're ghosting. We were just kids, but everyone's a kid at some point. So that doesn't let any of us off the hook, now does it?

I decide on the cheaper jalapeño poppers even though I know they're not as good. The peppers not nearly hot enough, the cream filling uselessly cool. All the cat ladies and lonely men have checked out long ago so it's just me now and the jingle bells and this microwave-safe garbage I don't even really want. And as I walk out through the grocery's automated doors, in that space where the empty shopping carts collect, I'm blasted with a wave of too hot air like under a hairdryer the size of the moon, so a second later when I step out into the crisp January night, my stomach flops and my lungs kind of burn. There's a second when I can't really see and I think, sure enough, my uncle and I would make a great team, swooning and faint in a rush of too much. But the truth is, I can't really ever lose my head the way I want to. Not again. My little diesel hatchback's the last car left in the lot and it's far, far away past all those domes of orange light glittering over every unused spot. There's road salt and black ice and everything locked inside a frost that's convinced it won't ever thaw. And I have to cross that space. I can't kid myself as to what can and can't be had. Arc lamps won't ever be the same orange as our tent. There'll never be enough Thursday nights to pay back all the rounds you're owed. Because memory is a debt with its own black interest, proving all distances are finite yet impossible to span. You and I both know, it'd be better if they had no end. Walking to my car with my hands full of nothing I want, I swear, it's forever before I'm there.

UNDER THE WING

After all the ugliness at the office over the politics of haircuts and presentability and how he ultimately loses his job, Cuthbert has to make a few stops—the after-school program where he volunteers, the hardware store and craft supply shop—before going home. It strikes him as funny while he navigates his city's streets, avoiding traffic and dodging pedestrians, that he should be in any sort of hurry. Does he not suddenly have all the free time he could possibly want? Cut loose from the obligations and responsibilities of work, is he not now free to pursue the remains of his life at a rate he enjoys and prefers? He even emptied his desk in a rush. Why wait? He resigns in person at the end of his session at the after-school program, then buys a length of rope, a cube of beeswax, and drives home.

The house Cuth rents is on the edge of a neighborhood of simple but sturdy houses, timber frames and stone foundations. Not so much the suburbs as what the suburbs reached to envelop. The sort of homes one would be more likely to find far out in the country, not just a few dozen blocks from town hall and the county courthouse. Beautiful old houses all done up with manicured yards. Tall trees and tire swings. Forsythia hedges ready to bloom. Cuth's place is at the end of a cul-de-sac: though the road continues on as a gravel scratch through some scrub and pines into a meadow strung up in high-voltage lines—the sort of ephemeral road used by the municipality for maintenance purposes alone—as far as Cuth or anyone else is concerned, this is the end of the line. Parking his car and gathering his purchases—breathing in the ripe early-spring air—Cuth stands in the cool stirring of last fall's leaves and new birds flitting among the bushes, among the trees, small piercing songs lacing through the afternoon's diminishing blue light. Then he mounts the porch stairs and steps inside.

This is the sort of place where a family is meant to live. Big kitchen. Big den. An upstairs full of bedrooms. An attic to store old toys, old clothes, an extra bed, an extra kid or cousin. If his sister and her daughter ever came down to visit, this would be perfect. They could stay forever and he'd never know. Somehow, they've never made the trip. The kitchen has two cast-iron skillets and a single aluminum pot for boiling water, a couple plates and knives and a ticking refrigerator, mostly empty. The den has a chair and an end table next to the chair and on the table: a book. Unread. Upstairs is a room with a typewriter perched on a stool. In another, a guitar leans against a folding metal chair. It has never struck Cuth as odd that he lives alone in such a huge empty space. A cathedral or a tomb. It has never struck him as odd that he'd want to.

In the back half of the house is what Cuth assumes an architect would call the Great Room. Large fireplace gone mostly unused. A bank of windows overlooking the back lawn and, beyond that, a dense stand of maple and birch. A ceiling vaulting high enough to create a sort of balcony or overlook of the second story's hall. Forming an X above everything, two heavy rough-sawn beams span the air to intersect and where they do, a large glass globe of lamp hangs from a chain. But Cuth's not interested in the light. It's those girders he's got his eyes on.

It takes a few attempts to toss the rope up and over the intersecting beams. Everything else follows with the ease of muscle memory: he's always been good with knots. He secures the rope to the X above by means of a simple gliding bowline, then waxes the remaining length to ensure an uninterrupted slip. He drags a chair in from the den and, on tiptoe, installs a classic thirteen-loop noose. Cuts the extra rope with a kitchen knife. Arranges his neck into the noose. He conducts these tasks with a sort of detached ambivalence. Efficiently, he is getting the work done. He plays with how teetery the chair is: pretty teetery. Then he just stands for a moment and stares out the bank of windows surrounding his cold fireplace. Grass, greening from grey. Bright buds on the tips of branches. The movement of birds. No regret or sorrow, no bitterness fluttering in his heart. Just the vague sense that it's all a waste. The white and purple splashes of crocuses sown wild throughout the yard. All of it's wasted on him. The wax on the rope smells nice.

"Not too bad," he says, and starts to tip over his chair, but in his pocket, his cell phone rings. Vibrates, actually, and chimes an electronic tinkling. He forgot to turn it off.

In this way, he is grateful that he paused long enough to admire the view. Briefly, he imagines swinging by his neck, the world fading, cooling but also somehow warming as if into sleep, while in his pocket something buzzes and sings. *Ting-a-ling-ling. Ting-a-ling-ling.* Cuth fishes the phone from his pocket to turn it off.

But it's Lindsay calling. The girl who manages the food co-op. Woman, really. Dark hair always dusted in a fine spray of flour. A baker. Always looking tired but also happy, maybe giddy with the weight of her exhaustion, most likely having been baking bread since long before the sun claimed the sky. He wonders if she's calling about his volunteer shift. Or perhaps he has a balance on his account. A minor debt unpaid. An oversight he should never have made. Pretty Lindsay with flour in her hair. Cuth flips open his phone and says hello.

"Hi Cuthbert. It's Lindsay."

"Hello Lindsay."

"How are you?"

Cuthbert looks down at himself standing atop his chair in the center of the room, strung to the girders, and shrugs. "I'm fine. Yourself?"

They talk for a few minutes. He precarious with the rope around his neck. She probably in her kitchen. Drinking tea. Flour in her hair. When he hangs up, they've made plans to meet for dinner in an hour.

It's hard work loosening the noose. Cuth puts the chair away in the den and goes upstairs to shower the wax flakes from his hair. He leaves the rope right where it is.

The restaurant where they meet is a sushi place where the customers all kneel at abbreviated tables, hanging lamps wrapped in brittle painted paper. Cuth is surprised at how comfortable he is on his knees. They eat small pieces of fish and drink hot sake and green tea, and they talk. She's a good talker. A good listener, too. He had not expected someone who works with her hands in the quiet dark of morning to know what a voice is for. He's glad that she does. It makes it easier to maintain his silence with her. Later, over small bowls of ginger ice cream, she asks him what the most incredible moment of his day had been—"What gave you pause, made you sit up and take notice of your life?"—and he has to admit, it's a pretty good question.

"After I was done work today," he says, looking off

vaguely past her, above her head and to the right, "I stopped at the place where I volunteer. It's a program for grieving children. Kids who've lost their parents. Mostly you just act as a friendly adult, you know, very casual, just make them feel safe and comfortable. So I was drawing pictures with this one little girl, and she's drawing a little horsy in pink and purple crayons, and when she's done she holds it up to me and says, 'Look, this is the mommy.'"

"Oh!"

"Then she ripped the picture in half and said, 'And this is the baby.'"

"Oh."

"I guess that was pretty good."

Throughout the restaurant, since before they arrived, there's been music softly playing. Like mournful birds in the rushes alongside some barely rippling pool. Songs older than sound. After a moment, Lindsay asks, "What were you drawing?"

And his answer: "Carrots." He scrapes his spoon along the empty bottom of his bowl. "Tons of them."

But later that night, while lying awake beside Lindsay in her warm bed, in her warm blankets and clean sheets and the clean scent of laundry and hair and girl, it's not the horsy he thinks of but his view from the noose. Greens and grays and splashes of purple, splashes of white. The tall naked trunks of trees and whatever lies beyond. All of it wasted on him. Hiding just behind his closing eyes. It's what he will think of every night that he lies beside her, every night for six more months until once again he sleeps alone and has lost what's left of his hair to time or to incident and has no one to talk to anymore but that great X in the air of his home, unchanging and unrelenting, negating everything beneath its twin wings.

PRETTY

He dumps the tin coffee can of unsorted keys out over the kitchen table. Then he drops the can on the floor. Outside I see the morning like a cold shred of wet rag snapping in the wind. It's not raining yet. But it's coming. Everything blue and building. He tells me to solve it myself.

A THIRTEENTH APOSTLE'S STAR

There's no exact measure to the emptiness of the desert between one barely extant town and another. Miles opening unto greater miles of flat brown shovel-breaking earth. Ringed in far off mountains. Oppressed by the never-ending downward press of sky.

Yet still: there are birds, circling. There are occasional crippled trees. Wicked thorns and arthritic habits. Sagebrush and weeds that give nothing back to the land. There's an arrow-straight line of railroad tracks cutting from one set of mountains to another, and there's a crumbling county road (numbered, not named) and where the two meet to form an X, a Ford pickup is jammed into the side of a ten car commuter train. Engine tipped over and derailed in the hardpan. A black plume of smoke marking where all these things meet. Funneling uninterrupted into the great blue palm above.

As of yet, no one's begun to scream. The silence that followed the tearing of metal—the woofing and flaring of fuel devouring—is almost more shocking than the preceding throttle and violence. The living don't know yet if they're dead. The dead don't need to know. For the moment, no one has begun to scream.

It's from this silence and swelling black smoke that Al emerges. Grey suit torn at the elbows. Right eye blood-blind from the gash tracing his fading hairline. He holds his head to keep the whole world from spinning away. He has no idea where he is. He sees the road and he sees the rail-line but neither means a thing. But the sun is a seething smirk. The unmoving air is a smirk but the crippled-tree shade is a kiss blown to him through the dead air, through the deathly light. Al stumbles away from the wreckage into the shade.

Somewhere far away, a sheriff's dispatcher gets a call. Someone somewhere sees smoke. Soon another call, and another: smoke in the desert. The dispatcher sends a cruiser out to investigate, though the poor kid has no idea where he's going. Head east until you see smoke. Head for the smoke. Finally, a call comes in from one of the train's passengers. Total hysterics. Insisting that everyone is dead. The dispatcher hangs up and sends out many more cars. Find the tracks. Look for smoke on the tracks. No one knows yet where they're going.

Before the sirens can be heard above the cries of the wounded and distressed, Al has wandered some distance from the wreck. Shambling from one pool of darkness to the next. Weaving between grey humps of sage. Stepping on tiny, tightly thorned cacti. Following the shadow-trail cast by the trees.

A quarter mile from the wreck, the trees lump into a tangled copse. Invitingly dark yet taunting in density. Al pushes through the lattice of deadwood and stems, discovers the trees' bright thorns. Softly sinking in. Only resisting when he tries to pull away. When he emerges on the other side, he no longer cares about cool or darkness. Only to escape the bite and sting.

It's in this state that he discovers the old woman. Hunching near her wheel-robbed caravan, kneeling in her pitiful garden. What are those horrible things, hairy-stalked and drooping heavy heads of curling, parched yellow? Sunflowers. She's kneeling among her sunflowers when he finds her. Sun shining off the fairly bald dome of her scalp. Shapeless dress like a sun-bleached curtain, almost floral, cinched around her waist with a man's leather belt.

Baring her teeth, the old woman raises one skeletal hand. Turns it at the wrist. Makes some parched and ancient sound with her throat.

Dumbstruck, Al takes his bloody hand from his head and waves back.

Once when he wasn't much younger, Al learned amazement at the swift changes a body can undergo, often in such short periods of time. How could something so helpless and small develop strong arms, a broad chest? How could blind, blinking eyes ease into seeing? The infant in the pictures could not possibly be the man he'd become. In high school, he could swim faster than any of the other boys. He could dance with girls and make them want to touch him. How could he have once been something else?

Yet even after all possible advantages have been attained, the body continues to change. His hair began to fall out. His waist took on a shape that made his legs somehow bird-like and gawky in comparison. The flesh of his neck thickened in unintended ways. There was nothing he could do about any of this. He could still make women want to touch him, and the women did touch him still, but they were changed, too. It depressed him to realize that he and everyone were helpless and had been from the start. And if he could look at his own life as a series of incomprehensible and uncontrolled physical changes leading to his disappointing yet still capable middle age, then what must this old woman feel as she rises and strides like some paralytic stork out from the dead or dying sunflowers and through the weeds to him, where her withered bone-trap hand takes his spotty and blood-smeared hand, where her myopic eyes squint at his bleeding brow as she asks him if he has something to do with that train wreck back over there?

Glancing over his shoulder, Al watches the black smoke billow and plume into the vapid blue. Blinks as the black expands, as the blue expands. Finally turns away.

"What train wreck?"

"Do you think he knew what he was doing?"

"I don't think he knew much of anything."

Calmly the father helps his teenage daughter out their train-car's window. Behind her, a pack of bodies waits to get out. But they're going to have to fend for themselves.

"I mean, maybe he thought he could beat the train." The language spoken between father and daughter is not the language of the other people on the train. "You know? Maybe get across the tracks before we did."

"Yeah, maybe." Taking his daughter's hand, the father leads her running to the shade of a nearby tree. "Or maybe he was drunk or on drugs or asleep."

"Maybe," she says as behind them, the first of countless strangers falls out of the window, landing badly on his shoulder, crying out among the other cries. "I guess he could have been asleep." Neither father nor daughter turns back.

The old woman's voice is high and reedy and incredibly dry sounding. Like two dead trees leaning against one another, groaning in night wind. Looking out toward the horizon, Al sees the entire world glimmering through a hazy screen. Shimmering sunflowers. Shimmering mountains. No matter how he tries, he cannot understand what she says. Finally, she tips her hand toward her mouth, and he gets it.

"Yes. A drink. Wonderful. Please. God bless you. God."

The first responders are not the first to respond. A miniscule stream of traffic backs up on either side of the wreck. Some people wait in their cars. Because there's air conditioning there, and satellite radio, too. A few get out to look, standing on the roadside, leaning at the waist as they stare. As if bending forward might give them a better view. After some time, a broken voice rises through a shattered window—

"Are you *doing* anything?"

—and given no other choice, the observers become involved. First a farmer and his young grandson. Then a truck driver on his way from Missoula to Sacramento. Yet even these people hesitate in their steps as alone with her two sleeping children in a sleek and spacious hatchback, a cow-eyed mother gradually comes to the conclusion that maybe the police should be involved. She finds her phone and dials 911. Plainly states where she is and what she sees. And now the dispatcher knows where all the cops and EMTs scattered seekingly throughout the desert should now, finally, be sent.

"What's your name, son?"

"Name?"

Somehow, through no logic or reason, he can understand her now, her withered mouth-sounds finally resolving into words. On paint-flaking chairs around a paint-flaking table, they're sitting in the caravan's shade, beneath the limp boughs of a tree. Leaves like long tickling fingers. Barely swaying. Al can't remember how he got here from the garden. Like time remained constant while space folded, erasing the gap between here and there. But wasn't that in a children's book?

"You know. What your mother called you."

Awfully technical for a children's book. On the small table between them, a glass sweats coolly between his hands, riding in a small pool of its own creation. He wipes a fingerful of moisture from the glass and rubs it into his eyes.

"Honestly, ma'am, I don't rightly recall at the moment."

"Then you shall be Laban." And she smiles. "You present yourself like a Laban."

"Great." Al sips and deduces his drink to be ice afloat in some sort of bourbon. On the table before the woman rests a can densely scripted in medical jargon. "Thank you." Unopened. "You going to join me? Or am I drinking by myself out here?" Somehow, the words feel familiar and welcome on his tongue. Like some holiday ritual. Repeated many times before.

Rearranging the lines of her face into some deathly sort of web, the old woman grins and checks her watch. "Give me ten minutes, okay?"

From far away, maybe one or both of them hears someone scream.

At the very rear of the train, there's a certain question among the passengers about what, exactly, is going on. Not long ago, they were drifting like a stream of bullets fired through the world. Now they're stopped. This is all they know. From their angle, they cannot see the smoke of the flaming pickup or the engine overturned on the ground. Large rocks block their view, and hunchback trees. Throughout the final car, there are whispered conversations as to what, if anything, they or someone else should do. The air conditioning has stalled along with their forward progress, and the automatic doors between cars have sealed shut. Something, obviously, must be done. People groan and throw their hands, wipe the sweat from their brows while near the back of the car, a couple in their mid-forties—a used car salesman and the secretary to a used-car salesman (a friendly competitor at the lot up the street)—quietly argue. She thinks that, if he gets off the train, they'll begin moving again and he'll be left behind. He's convinced (rightly, though for the wrong reasons) that this will not happen. They're each trying to use the narrow armrest in between them. Neither seems to think that the other is sharing enough.

"Trust me, babe," and smiling, he leans in to kiss her cheek. "It's going to be fine." And in the moment when their two fleshes touch, the salesman's wife hopes he's wrong. She hopes the train will pull away and leave him out here. She hopes the sun mercilessly cooks him into a pretentious, condescending cinder.

Pulling the emergency latch and slipping out through the opened window (it's not as easy as he thinks it should be), the secretary's husband starts to walk alongside the train, trying to match his step to the creosote-soaked ties. But his stride is unnatural and awkward. And above the scent of the sun-hot ties, something bad hangs in the air. And in the passing windows, pale faces look out at him, imploring, needing. So he jogs down the talus embankment, away from the tracks and into the hardpan and weeds. And now he sees the black finger of smoke accusing the open sky. And just past these hunchback trees bowing like leprous beggars, he can see the tipped engine and see the burning truck.

The secretary's husband likes to brag about his time in the service. He thinks this will endear his customers to him and maybe solidify a sale. But he was only ever a weekend reservist. Our war then was cold and if our enemy had ever struck, we'd all have died all at once anyway: the battle would have been everywhere in a sterilizing flash, then just as quickly, not been anywhere. The only mortal combat in which he ever engaged was with a thirty-pack in the back of a troop carrier, roving the peripheries of the SAC base in the ink and blotter mist before dawn. Nothing he's done or claimed to know has prepared him for the flames and torn metal, the crying figures dragging themselves out of broken windows, the still bodies spread out on the ground. He stands and watches while his insides turn into a cold and syrupy fluid. Then he rushes back to his wife. It's imperative: he must return to his wife.

Before the flames boiled to peel its paint away, the pickup was a pale baby blue. Fenders rusted to a coxcomb orange. A red and black NRA decal crooked in the rear window. The train an industrial grey with a blue stripe running its length. The windows all tinted black.

Cracked desert clay the same faded ochre as a desiccated orange rind. Baked beyond life in the sun. The sagebrush is grey. The leaves of the track-side trees all silvery green.

The tracks are gunmetal black, the ties a deep tar-stained brown. The smoke is an opaque ashy smudge.

And amid the dead grey weeds and deadly greying sunflowers, the caravan is a washed out red and gold. The windows are aged with flyshit and dust. Over the door, a punched tin star hangs by an eight-penny nail.

And the old woman's skin is a burnt and leathery red. Wisps of hair fishing-line white. Her eyes a clear piercing blue. From her neck by a shining gold chain, an ornate crucifix is poised and for Al—all pale skin and blonde hair and torn up slate-grey seersucker—this last detail is a strange revelation. He had not noticed the cross before. The colors of the world come together into a broken vision of dirty stained glass, Dead Sea lost, and at its center, a golden dead man hangs in suspended tribulation from a polished golden cross.

Al sips amber off the melting ice in his glass. The old woman checks the black ticking hands of her watch, and sighs.

Back before his body continued past the apex of its progression, Al spent a summer on a recently-abandoned farm. The sun-stained shapes of missing pictures burned in the wallpaper. Clothes still scattered in drawers, on the floor. The water and electric still ran, at least at first, and the fields were still orderly yet totally gone to seed, an occasional stray and lost-eyed cow wandering through. It was the summer between semesters and he lived in a ghost farm with a woman whose body was a candle flame eating up the wick of his heart. Did he meet her here in this big empty place? Did she follow him here from school? Perhaps he was the one who followed her. They spent their days reading books in the sun, in the wind, on the porch or in the soft susurrus of bending wild grass. He remembers the sound of her laugher as her body opened like praying hands. He remembers a wind-chime on the corner of the porch. Tolling three notes like the suggestion of a beginning or end. Tolling one note three times. Tolling one note just once.

But really what he remembers is the night they pushed a mattress out of the extra bedroom's second-story window. How it bounced and cartwheeled across the yard. It was the longest day of the year, or anyway, the latest the sun would set. They dragged the mattress into the tall grass and spread out a soft moth-holed quilt over top. The nodding wheat heads formed a frame above them: in all the world, there was only the mattress and the grass and the box of sky overhead, slowly turning from deep pink to purple to black, filling impossibly with an unending wash of stars, brightly winking planets, an eventual god-like slice of sterling, blinding moon. There was nothing else in the whole world. Not even the two of them, watching. Least of all the two of them.

Whatever happened to that girl, he wonders now in the shade beside the caravan. He can't even recall her face. Just her long blonde hair. The arc of her hips. Her voice like the first cold sip of beer on a hot night. He wonders if maybe he married her or if maybe she got away. He looks at his hand for evidence of a ring—a faint indentation, a discolored band—but the blood he now wears obscures whatever proof he might seek.

For a moment, he wonders where the blood came from. Then: he remembers. Somewhere far behind him, a siren faintly sounds. Watching him observe his own hands, the old woman smiles silently to herself, then after a moment digs around inside her dress to produce a leather-bound book. Deep red and no bigger than a cigarette pack. Creased and worn as if by centuries of earth-dirty callused hands.

"Let me read to you something, Laban," she says, thumbing through the nearly translucent pages. "I think to you this might somehow apply."

The sight and sound of the open book fills Al with a sick sense of unease. Like a snake all curled up in the dank cave of his belly. Ready to unfurl.

And she reads:

After these things, the Autogenes said, "Let the twelve angels come into being so that they might rule over the chaos and the oblivion." And behold an angel appeared from the cloud whose face was pouring forth fire, while his likeness was defiled with blood. And he had one name, "Nebro," which is interpreted as "apostate," but some others call him "Ialdaboath" . . . Nebro then created six angels to attend him. And these produced twelve angels in the heavens, and each of them received an allotted portion of the heavens. And the twelve rulers, along with the twelve angels, said, "Let each one of you . . . "

"But the rest of the scripture," she says, pausing to clear her throat, "is lost."

"Well," Al says, "isn't that something." But this idea—angels creating angels to give shape and dominion to and over the earth and heaven—does not click with Al's understanding of the world. For there are beautiful coastal mountains plunging headlong into the sea. There are towering trees and hills teeming with life. Birds in the sky and fish in the rivers. Everywhere all at once. Yet there's also this: an empty dead expanse of nothing at the center of the world. Every inch identical to the inch before and after. The whole middle of the country, he knows, is like this: unshaped and unformed, a flat and undifferentiated plain. Just like Russia. Just like Australia. Where is there any evidence to prove that God did not simply give up? An entire infinite system of burning gases spinning around burning gases, and our tiny blue planet enthroned with the universe revolving worshipfully around it. But God gave up. Moved the center somewhere else. Left His failure behind. For every ounce of His divine soul He poured into our creation—every mountain and every forest, each tree and antelope and butterfly and monkey—every last detail His attempt at perfection, and each one a monument to failure. The overspecialization of the giraffe and koala, any other marsupial or monotreme. The obscene vulnerability of the manatee and every human male's exposed and flaccid genitals. Unable to make real what His mind envisioned, the Great and Unknowable Failure turned away from His unfinished and dismal masterwork, abandoning His failed creations to cope in their failed, imperfect home.

The old woman closes her book and grins. "So many busy hands!" and laughs. A singularly horrible sound.

When the police and ambulances and fire trucks finally arrive, the evacuation is already well underway. Once the shock of having survived set in, people began leaking out of the wreck, automatically knowing only to save themselves. When the secretary's husband returned from his scouting, the other passengers in the rear-most car—rattled but generally unscathed—poured out the windows, kicked open the emergency exits, rushed to the front to help the other survivors free. Near the front, where the flames of impact were spreading—eager and fierce as cannibals to consume—an elderly man cradles the ruined body of his wife of fifty-three years. They were enjoying a late morning bagel with cream cheese, some coffee. Then the engine tipped over and she was dashed into their café car table. Now her body's like a limp sack holding the splintered dust of her bones. He presses her bloodied brow to his mouth, to his cheek, holds what's left of her close. The flames dance and lick around him and someone shouts through an open door for him to move, c'mon, let's go. But eventually, the shouting stops. The old man closes his eyes and waits for his chance to let go while outside, a pregnant woman in a pretty blue dress squats down with her back against a stone and wails into the dead air, hugging her belly above the blood staining the ground beneath her. Children wander and cry out to their parents who may or may not hear or respond. Men and women seek out their partners, their children, their friends. Red Cross volunteers hand out blankets, uselessly. A helicopter arrives and dumps a spray of retardant chemicals on everyone. And in his pickup, the man responsible for all of this curls more tightly around the steering wheel, blackened and growing blacker. Somehow all of this Al knows without seeing. The fluid through which all light must pass. In the superheated sky, the rising plume finally succeeds in eclipsing the sun, leaving the survivors to toil in the apocalyptic shade while a quarter-mile away—in a waste of sunflowers and locusts and olives, at the very end of the line—Al finishes his drink as the old woman slowly unbuttons her shirt to reveal a plastic tube and funnel stretching out from a bandage on her softly distended belly. Breasts like deflated honeydew. Funnel and tube cloud-stained dirty with use. Opening the can on the table before her with one long and yellowed fingernail, the old woman holds it up with her pinky daintily jutting—

"Bless this bounty."

—and pours her breakfast directly inside. And for a moment, Al has to wonder—in the absence of all other knowledge, his family and past, his own pitiful and meaningless name—if maybe he's the man inside the burning pickup, hands clutching tight the mechanism of his mistake as his eyes melt out from the grottoes of his skull, as his mouth falls open to shatter and split like driftwood, like glass, as the flames lovingly lick as the most delicate lover the ringed knuckles of his spine.

FRAISES DES BOIS

He parks the truck at the edge of a rutted field road, wild hyssop and solidago bowing beneath tire and grill. There are clouds that move like spun-steel galaxies and between the clouds: deep blue. A meadow of wild prairie grass stretches beyond the roadside weeds while far along past that, some apple trees run a ragged line. The man steps out of his father's pickup and listens for a moment to the engine's cooling tick. Breathes the green pungency of crushed weeds underfoot. The scent of field and sun and hot motor. With the wind stirring through the grass, this hilltop feels like the final pointing fingertip of the world. Stepping past the weeds into the meadow, he recalls: it always has.

In his memory there is a path here. Here or somewhere nearby. But now it is only meadow. Tall whispering green and swishing brown, nodding tasseled heads. The sound is a mockingbird's song of the ocean. A sea of dry and slender tongues.

From where he left the truck, he could see the tall willow tree bending languidly toward the ground, and beyond that, just the shape of the house's gambrel. Now, growing closer, he can see much more. The sag and lean of the ell. The windows as vacant eyes. Missing shingles and rotten claps. Where once there was a garden and long lawn, the meadow runs straight up to the porch. All at once, it seems fitting as well as a shame. He mounts the played-out steps and crosses the porch, walks in through the open door.

Certain things, he'll decide, aren't necessary anyway. The dust-mouthed faucet above a basin stained with rust. Dead switches. Wallpaper peeling at the corners, along the seams. Animals have lived here. But animals have always lived here. In an upstairs room, he looks out a window, sees apple trees running in a line into the distance, dividing two tracts of wild, grassy land. He crosses the upstairs and looks out an opposing window: property-line orchard, wild fields on either side. It's what he expected—world repeating without error—but he knows he could have gone his whole life without that confirmation. It does him no good to see. The man walks through the last rooms of the house, takes stock of what remains, what is gone, then goes outside to the porch to sit in a weather-grey Adirondack chair.

"This is yours now," he says, watching the night's approach sap the light from the vacuous sky. "No one but you."

He sits until it is dark. He sits for a while more after that. Listening to the night sounds' rise and fall. Later, he creeps inside, following the light of a dozen successive matches upstairs into a room where a mattress has been left flopped naked on the floor. The man strips down in the dark and folds his clothes and sleeps. Still surrounded by the songs of the night.

Should he have expected something less or something more? The man isn't sure. In the morning, he dresses before a clouded, speckled mirror hanging from the back of a closet door. Leans in. Inspects his reflection, his face, his hands.

"That's not you," he whispers. To the greying stubble. To the wrinkles surrounding his eyes. Then he says it again, more forcefully: "Get out of my house."

It's cool and dewy yet when Susan steps out into the morning and among the woods sloping down behind her house, up through high fields and into a nubbled meadow. She carries a basket made of woven dogwood twigs. In the basket rests a stained towel, folded over a sealed jar of hot coffee.

This meadow is not hers or her dad's—it belongs to the Kellogg family, whose homestead lies nearly a mile to the east—but that doesn't matter. She's on good terms with the Kelloggs, and anyway, she's come here for years and never once seen another human soul. So it might as well belong to her. But she doesn't think of it this way. With the morning sun warming her back, Susan kneels and bends over the low groundcover, preens the leaves to fill her basket with a harvest of wild strawberries.

To Susan, the work is merely work. She's not aware of thinking anything while she does it.

She pauses once mid-morning to drink her jar of coffee. While she rests, she watches a bald eagle circle high above in perfect, unerring glides. It's searching. But it does not dive. No mice today, Susan thinks. Too bad. It looks like real work, how it flies away on the force of its massive, articulate wings. She finishes her coffee and gets back to her harvest.

The strawberries here are plentiful but small. It's impossible to fill her basket. She knows: what she gathers will be plenty. When she's tired and finger-stained enough to consider her job done, she stands and stretches, folds the towel to cover the berries and gathers up her basket but decides to take a different route home, a longer path through two overgrown parcels of land that no one's been able to buy up. A line of ancient apple trees parses the tracts, weeds and wild grass on either side. Susan walks this orchard line. Basket-handle arcing through the crook of her elbow, one hand resting gently along her belly's flat plain. When the abandoned Jennings farm comes into view, she thinks she sees someone out where the dooryard might once have been. From this distance, it's just a shape and some movement. So she gets closer to see.

At the house, the man has stomped down the tall grass between the porch and the old well pump. He's working the complaining handle to fill a tin pail with water when he sees her approaching through the grass. Just as she could see him for a distance: he's been watching her come for a while. Hoping he's wrong but knowing that he's not. It's a long moment after they've each met eyes before slowly, he raises one hand, and waves.

His is an unease to already have a guest. He invites her inside anyway for coffee. After waking this morning, he soaked his jeans in dew walking through the tall grass to fetch his father's pickup. Drove slowly through the field to establish a new driveway. Coursed a careful circuit around the house to mark a makeshift yard before parking and unloading an Army bag of clothes and a banana box of provisions. Now, in his house, he starts a fire in the woodstove and fills a camp kettle with water from the well. The woman sets down her basket on the dirty kitchen table among faded receipts and scattered dead leaves, then sits in one of two wooden chairs. It creaks.

"I'm a little bit bashful," he says, "about having someone see this place in the state it's in." But by how he says this, it's obvious it isn't true. He'd earlier swept the floors with a length of willow bough cut from the tree outside, then gathered up most of the scattered trash, but still the house smells of animal and weather. It seems pretty clear that he feels fine about this. It'll be a long time, Susan thinks, before the inside feels very much different from the outside.

"I was coming home from picking strawberries when I saw you out in the yard," she says. Then her pale eyes grow large as she gestures to her basket. "Have some, if you like."

The man nods and helps himself to a handful. Then another. "These are good." He isn't lying. This whole time, he's been standing by the stove, but now, mouth full, he wipes his hands clean on the thighs of his jeans and bends to fetch two tin cups from the banana box on the floor, dumps coffee grounds from a can into each, splashes in hot water from the stove. He's still chewing when he passes her a cup, gesturing in a way that suggests an apology: he wishes the coffee were more.

"Thank you."

And again: the gesture. He's still chewing. But he's sitting now and seems pretty relaxed in his blue work shirt and jeans. He lifts one leg and crosses it over the other. Into the wooden back of his chair, he leans.

"So you live here now?"

And finally: he swallows.

"The house is mine, yes."

Sweetness tingling down his throat.

"But not for very long?"

"I got in just last night."

But that wasn't what she was trying to say.

"I was a little girl the last time I remember anybody living up here. I live across the way on a parcel my dad sold me, down the road a piece from my dad's place." She points vaguely westward. The man thinks: she could be pointing anywhere. But he knows. "I can hardly remember what the last folks raised up here." And now she's the one who's lying. The land is bordered all around in long strands of apple trees, and within the trees lie tracts of loamy pasture and field. Good land. She remembers, in those pastures, many horses. Their dark shapes impressed against the blue sky.

Across from her, the man sips his coffee and shrugs. "Who knows!" And now he's complicit in her lie.

The woman does something with her coffee, then sets it down. Folds her hands in her lap. Watches them worry the fabric of her faded sundress. Then she reaches her hand into the basket's folded towel and carries a red handful to her mouth. It's clear in how she does this, it's what she's wanted all along. An impulse beyond hunger: she wants. The man watches her, watches the animal satisfaction she gets from eating strawberries, and it's a soft blue feeling that comes with the realization that she's not pretty. Too many freckles and too skinny and teeth a little crooked. She's almost pretty. Which is worse than if she were ugly.

Outside, the wind is doing something to the overgrown meadow. It would seem that the meadow likes what the wind does. There are animals out there that neither the man nor the woman can see. These animals are surviving.

When Susan leaves a little while later, she makes a motion like she's going to touch him. He does not move into or away from her touch. But in the end, it's like she's brushing soot from his sleeve, and she's gone.

It was nice seeing Susan again, he later thinks while chopping wood behind the house. Rounds flying off as twin splits beneath the axe's head. Even still, he hopes she doesn't come back.

He remembers his father as the scent of hay and coffee, his hands as the bark of hard trees. He remembers lying on his back in the hayfields to watch the sky-vault above and later gathering that same hay into bales. The swing of an axe making a tree into fuel. His father oiling leather, just a dim working shape within the shadows of the barn. The autumn smell of turning apples. Golden rod and milkweed plumes. All of these things are his father. They would lead the horses slowly into trailers to take to other farms or sometimes would ride the horses there if the farm was near enough. They'd watch the horses gambol and couple and rear. Then they'd bring their horses home. He remembers, deep in the belly of one green pasture, a pond of the coldest spring water. He remembers—each of them howling beneath the summer sun—his father throwing him in.

ADVENTURE STORIES FOR MEN & BOYS

A moose lifts its head from among the brush and reeds banking an icy algae-green stream. Antlers like some ancient god's open, skyward claws. Eyes like pink jewels set in its washed-out, near-white fur: ice rotting under a spring sun, snow clinging to a mountain face. The moose raises its head—beard and bell dripping, stiffening with ice from where it's been browsing in the stream—and its improbable eyes meet your eyes, locking like shudders, locking like bolts, and from a distance of under one hundred feet, perhaps for the first time in your life, you are seeing and being seen.

What do you do?

If you're a gang of good old boys out in the Buxton woods, of course, you shoot a round from your .30-06 through the thickly swaying flesh of its throat. Watch it drop in a heap before you, gushing red and choking on itself. Wait for the choking to stop. Drag its body through the crisply shouting January snow, load it up and drop it off at the local tagging station, a convenience store off of Route 117. Leave it for the storeowner, Dale Cummings, to sort out. It is Wednesday and barely past the first dawn of the new year and Dale stands in the diminishing snarl of tires against frost-tight gravel, watching the last faint helix of steam curling up from the angry red gash. Dale has fought in Korea and fought in his kitchen and he's no longer of an age where he feels prepared for these sorts of things. You try to be good and try to do right. Yet the shit always piles up, often on fire, right outside your door. Dale leaves the still-warm carcass where it lies in the parking lot gravel, steps inside his store and dials up the game warden's office in New Glouster.

One would hope it's too early for anything to have already gone wrong. Lonnie takes the call when it comes in, nods and *mm-hmm*s while tugging a dark curl tucked behind her ear, then puts the call through to Warden Ellis who, one wall and four steps away, picks up and listens, receiver cradled between neck and shoulder, pen in hand hovering above a notepad, but what's there to remember? Almost nothing. A body. A location. A lack of perpetrator or anything resembling evidence. At his elbow, a styrofoam cup of black coffee grows cold and stale, a foamy ring of scum clinging to the margins. Warden Ellis hangs up and stands, empties the cup swiftly and without tasting, steps out of his office and to the coat rack by Lonnie's desk.

"Heading down to Buxton or Hollis," he says, wrestling into his coat. "Whichever. The tagging station down at Dale Cummings's store." Errant drops of coffee cling to his mustache hairs. "Some kids shot a moose and dumped it in his lot."

Like she doesn't know. Particleboard paneling and a fragrant carpet. This place has never been too big for them.

"Seems rather pointless, all that work." She doesn't look up when she speaks: she's reading something. "Waiting and aiming and shooting and dragging. And for what?" What's that she's got? "Why bother?"

"Is that a comic book?"

"A trade paperback," like he should know better. Lonnie shows him the cover, shadowy figures dissolving into shadowy scenes. Passion and violence or maybe violence disguised as love. A comic book.

"It's an albino."

Lonnie cocks her head like any sort of animal. She's lost. "The suspect?"

"The moose."

She sets down her book. "That's something else altogether, huh?"

The two of them have been working together out of this tiny office for over a decade. A proximity of bodies and years and seconds. Ellis keeps wondering when she'll finally start to feel like more than a surrogate kind of sister.

"Maybe they got spooked. Didn't realize what they were poaching until it was too late." He's got his coat on now. Why is he dithering? "I'll be back before noon."

"You hope."

"I hope. I do."

Once Ellis took a trip out to New York State to visit his brother. It was February and before he left, he'd tossed an orange into the cab of his truck, something to eat on the long trip down, but of course he forgot all about it until he was heading back home later that same day. It was night and freezing and the orange was solid as a stone, hard and pitted like something from space, rimed lightly in pale frost. That's what the world reminds him of today as he slips through New Glouster and onto I-95 south, the pavement frosted grey, the leafless trees frosted grey, the sunlight and sky frosted grey. He exits near the Macchigone Jetport and takes Route 22 out past the farms and lumberyards, the nurseries all buttoned up tight for the winter, into the deepening woods, pulls onto Route 117 and pulls up to Dale's store where Dale is waiting for him, standing outside with his breath erupting like smoke from a furnace—impossible plumes, so much greater than anything he could possibly contain—and there it is, spread out at Dale's feet like the worst kind of news. Horn and hoof and flanks of dirty white. It makes Ellis's stomach sour and tight just to see it.

Dale gives a feeble wave as the warden pulls in, parking the truck between the body and the road. He doesn't want to attract any more attention than necessary. Stepping out into the cold and wind, he tries to make a joke, something about the ex-wife bitterness of the weather, but it's like Dale can't even hear him. And maybe he can't. Ellis has to acknowledge, it might be better that way.

"Them sonsabitches. Such a goddamned shame." Dale stands with his hands balled and spit frozen in beads to his white beard, and he's shaking. It's not entirely clear if it's only from the cold. "Taking down something so goddamned rare as this, and for what? Not for any greater purpose. Not for a freezer full of steaks. Fucks up our day, Warden."

Ellis nods, but isn't listening, is kneeling down beside the body, inspecting the wound, touching the fur. More notable to Ellis than the tarnished whiteness of its coats, its rack is a misshapen nest of hooks and spurs. Less like supplicant palms. More like grasping hands.

"Our day is fucked, this bull is dead, and to what end, Warden?"

"Well, what you're saying," as he peers at its haunches, "is only partly of a truth," and he points.

Dale squints. Then hunkers down. Gets as close a look

as he can.

"Huh."

"Ever seen anything like that before?"

"What's there to see? Ain't a thing there."

Between its legs, a furry nothing where its loins should be. A faint ureic stain. That's all.

"Fairly common where incest's concerned." Ellis stands, walks around the animal. "A bull mounts his daughter and sires a eunuch." Crouches near the gun wound. "Born neuter." The warden strokes the moose's rent neck, strokes its meaty nose. "Same with the antlers. And the albinism."

"Goddamn."

Ellis sniffs and wipes at his nose. "Not common of course. I mean, the odds are… But when it happens, this is what you get."

For a moment, both men crouching by this dead animal, the world draws to a stillness. No traffic passing. No wind to bite. Everything briefly condensed into a single pure cell. Then the warden speaks.

"You have any idea who did this?"

He stands to regard the man next to him. Dale is shorter than Ellis, and wiry. Like he's been scrapping all his life.

"No sir." Chin up. Chest forward.

"You're sure."

"I heard a racket and came on out and there it was all

laid out on the ground and that damn pickup riding away."

"And you didn't recognize the boys who did it?"

"No sir."

"And you didn't recognize the truck?"

Dale smiles like he's agreeing to have a tooth pulled. "What would you have me do, Warden? Say I do know them boys. Then what? See them go to jail? See their families suffer? Maybe they just get a fine. Something more than they can ever pay. It don't matter. They know I'm the one with the body. If anything comes of it, they'll know right where it come from."

"They're the ones that left it here, Dale. They know your position, that this is a tagging station."

"Point is, Warden, I *don't* know them. And if I did, I'm certain the law can't fix what's happened here. No fine or sentence can make this thing alive again." But for the wind tossing the frayed edges of his beard, the old man stands perfectly still while he speaks. "The world is a snake eating its own tail. Them boys *will* get theirs." He's not even wearing a coat. "It don't need to be a state issue."

Early on in this line, Ellis learned: there is being a representative of your state and its edicts, and there's being a person among people. One cannot reconcile with the other. Where does procedure fit in? This body will have to be taken to Augusta. It will need to be examined. It will probably end up in the hands of some taxidermists, then eventually in the State House or in a museum. From the moment the bullet left the chamber, it's been a state issue. But Ellis says none of this.

"Help me get it in the truck."

By now, a few folks who've stopped at the store to buy gas or coffee or cigarettes have taken notice. Ellis backs the pickup around and drops the tailgate and two young guys trot over to help. They grapple hold of legs and hide, count and heave and the body doesn't rise or land with much grace, but the warden suspects that grace has never had much to do with death. Everyone tumbles like a string-cut puppet. Everyone shits their pants. He once heard that the men being led to execution have to wear diapers for this reason. Where's the dignity in that? Being gassed to death in a diaper. Before a firing squad, blindfolded, in a diaper. Ellis thanks the boys for their help, then rolls out a canvas tarp over the body and ties it down. Latches the tailgate. Shakes hands with Dale in the sharp morning light and drives away, leaving the old man alone with his store and his fists and a near-black pool congealing on the ground.

Warden Ellis doesn't get far before digging out his cell phone and calling his office, updating Lonnie on the details of the situation.

"We're probably going to want to get the boys on top involved."

"Yeah, that's a likely assumption." Lonnie sounds tired. "Shall I give them a ring?"

"If you would." Even so early on these vacant holiday roads, there are still now and then cars ahead of or behind or passing him. Who are these people? Why aren't they home? Why aren't they sleeping? "Did you have a good time out last night?"

"Oh, it was fine. Hung around at my sister's until midnight, then headed for home."

"She having a party?"

"A party is what it was."

Heading the opposite direction, a sheriff's cruiser passes Ellis. They wave.

"I'm sorry, Lonnie. I should have given you the day off today."

"Like everyone else in the world?"

"Like everyone else in the world."

He wants to offer her the rest of the day off. But he needs her. He can't fix this situation on his own.

"Get a hold of the boys in Augusta, then call me back. Let me know if I'm heading up there directly or back to the New Glouster station first."

"Sure thing, Warden."

He could make her his wife, probably. Or maybe at least just live together for a while. It could be fun. He's certain, he would take good care of her.

"As soon as this is over, I swear I'll make it up to you."

"You better."

"I will." And he believes it, too.

Driving back to Maine through the ink-black New York night, crossing state lines, Ellis held the frost-stiff orange to his lips, breathing hotly until a soft spot in the rind emerged. Then he bit a hole through the skin and nursed the frozen meat, coaxing out the juice and flesh, one cold drop at a time.

There are incidents of bodies and incidents of gravity and sometimes they're the same thing. Back in Macchigone, the highway cloverleaf is closed. In the hour or so that the warden spent negotiating the animal's carcass, a cement truck from Auburn overturned at the base of the off-ramp, spilling hot concrete all over the pavement. No one can get through until the mess has been cleaned. Ellis bypasses the accident and finds a detour, drives further into the outskirting industrial territories around Macchigone— donut shops and gas stations, towering medical facilities and a single sparkling-new commuter rail yard—until he can merge onto 295. It's not the highway he wants, but it will get him where he needs to go. All obstacles have paths that supersede.

Meanwhile, the tarp behind him snaps violently. It's a bad habit of his, never tying it down tightly enough. A man in his profession, he is certain, should not be so bad with knots. He makes it through the city and now the highway is picking up pace—he is driving through the frozen salt marshes of Falmouth, a meandering paisley of ice shouldered in humps of frosted grass, tufting like mussed hair—and he cranes his head around to check the tarp (still good) but as he's turning back to face forward, he sees something off the highway. Amid the paisley ice. Among the humping grass. Just a glimpse, something pale and pink. It's his job to stop, but that's not why he does. Warden Ellis pulls off the highway onto the shoulder's crunching ice and snow. Clicks on his hazard lights. Leaves the engine running and heads out into the marsh.

In the warmer months, this is a tidal creek ribboning eventually into the bay. Slow and deliberate. Sometimes flowing backwards. Beyond the marsh stands a copse of denuded swamp maple and poplar, then the opening mouth of Casco Bay. Eider ducks bobbing on the surface. Crows or seagulls slowly circling. All sorts of things unseen beneath the water's face, and Ellis cannot see that pale shape anymore. Not a glimpse amid the dormant earth, the frozen creek. He remembers, though, vaguely where it was. Crossing the marsh's banks, fording the ice when necessary, the warden cuts as straight and true a path as possible, and when he finds the littered clothes on the stomped-down grass and finally finds the man, naked and submerged in a hole punched through the ice, not so much pink now as blue, he isn't all that surprised. Ellis kneels down and grapples with the man, hooks first an armpit, then an arm, drags the body out of the water and onto the ground. Chances are, he meant to drown. The shock of the water convinced him to hold his breath. The warden slaps the man to get his eyes open, to get his lungs inflating less sluggishly, and as the man's head lolls from side to side, disoriented, seeking, Ellis can see that, though young, this man is going bald. But why should he notice this? Of all the things. The few patches of hair the man has left have been shaved, but still: the stubble forms a map of strange continents across his skull.

There's no point in trying to dress him out here: Ellis takes off his heavy coat and wraps it around the man, lifts up his wet and freezing body, carries him through the marsh. Settles him in the passenger seat of the truck. Cranks the heat on high.

"You got a name, son?"

"..."

"Is there anyone with you?"

"..."

"I'm going to go get your clothes. I'll be right back."

The man keeps his eyes closed, chin to chest, seems to be nodding to himself. As if listening to a lesson he understands and should have already known. Ellis backtracks through the marsh to fetch the man's clothes.

The ice here is fairly thick. Ellis is certain, if he

searched, he'd find a large stone directly beneath the hole. On the bank alongside, Ellis gathers up the scattered clothes. Searches the pockets. No wallet. No keys. Nothing. In the inside pocket of the jacket, Ellis finds a security badge for an engineering firm that he knows went under last year. Something about a lawsuit, employees feeling harassed, et cetera. In the badge's photograph, the man still has his hair. It's clear that soon it will all be gone. Beside the photo is an employee number and barcode and the unlikely name Cuthbert Grant. Ellis fingers the ID and wonders who would do that to their child, bestow an awkward historical name so clearly over the heads of almost anyone he might ever meet.

In the front pocket of the jacket, Ellis finds a comic book rolled into a tube. From what he can glean from skimming its pages, it's a noir-story about a writer who's given himself wholly to the characters born of his own imagination. It's called *The Book of Hours*. Looking out across the ice and grassy dunes to the highway and his truck and the man slumped inside, Ellis cannot imagine who this man might be.

Above the highway, a plastic shopping bag catches in the limbs of a winter grey poplar, shushing and flailing in the wind. The warden helps the man dry off and get dressed and get back into the now hot pickup cab. Beyond that, he's at a loss. No other cars parked on the highway shoulder. No address on the ID. Not a word from the man himself.

"Is there any place you'd like to go?"

"..."

"I'm legally obligated to take you to a hospital."

"..."

"Heap of trouble."

Ellis takes the man out for an early lunch. What else is there to do? He pulls the truck back onto the highway and takes the nearest exit, stops at a diner with a neon sign and mirrors running the length of the counter. The illusion of greater spaces. The man follows Ellis without speaking, without looking up, slumps into a corner booth and fiddles with the silverware.

When the waitress arrives, gum-snapping and youthfully bored, Ellis orders a coffee and a grilled cheese with tomato.

"My friend here'll have the same."

She raises her eyebrows in a parody of surprise while taking down the order on her pad, then leaves. From where they are sitting, they can see no windows. Most of the patrons are obscured. Even the mirrors are no help. They have nothing but one another.

"Your ID says you're Cuthbert Grant."

"..."

"Did your parents mean that as some sort of joke?"

The man turns over one hand, moves it slowly away. It seems like that sort of gesture should mean something, but somehow Ellis doubts it.

The waitress brings their coffees, is gone again. He wonders why she should be so surly, so unhappy, then remembers: it's a holiday. Working today has ruined the night before. Why is he the only person in this whole world unconcerned with the date? The warden looks around the diner to get a look at the patrons—their heft or sag, the weight of their lives and the grace with which it's carried—but still, he can't make out anything about them. There are some days, he can see for miles. An eagle on a moss-hoary limb. A man slipping under river ice. Why can't he see now?

"There was this time a while ago when I was visiting my brother in New York State." It's strange, he thinks, how this keeps occurring to him, this one episode. "It was about this time of year, maybe later, and when I showed up at his place, he weren't there. Still at work or something, I supposed. So I waited for a while, then went for a walk out in the woods behind his house. I got pretty deep out there, too, not really paying any attention. This was around the same time my wife had decided to leave me, so I suppose I had a lot on my mind. Distracted. I only say so because when I came out of the woods at the pond, I took it to be a meadow or pasture of some kind. Just a big open area covered in snow. Didn't think nothing of it until suddenly I was two feet shorter and soaked through up past my knees. I remember it being like a slap, or like somebody'd just shaken me awake. A reset button. Everything before that was a kind of walking coma. Then all at once"—and he claps his hands together—"I'm awake."

The man is staring down at the table. After a moment, the waitress slides a sandwich in front of him. So now he's staring at a sandwich.

"I'm going to wager a guess," the warden says, "that's not how you feel right now."

But maybe this is what he's been hoping for. Maybe this is what he meant. This man is named Cuthbert and this man looks up at him with his jaw set and his mouth firm, ice-chip eyes meeting Ellis's and locking in. It's just like he's falling through.

"I'm not usually one to say such things," and his voice is like a shovel into rough earth, "but your loneliness is a poison."

"Well sir, that—"

"You're a man with a dead moose in his pickup." He pauses long enough for his statement to sink in. "You're cruising around the countryside scraping the dead up off the side of the road so you can take it all home with you. Make it warm. Buy it dinner." Ever so slightly, Cuthbert leans forward. So slightly, the warden leans away. "And you expect *me* to somehow identify with *you*?"

It's like watching a zeppelin fill up into its fullness, the slowness with which Cuthbert rises from and leaves the table. And maybe there's been a third option, too. Maybe those boys in the Buxton woods knew exactly what they were seeing. Something rare and finite. Something no one else would likely see again. Unless they intervened.

From where he is sitting, the warden cannot see Cuthbert leave. So he stands. He wants to tell him about the fear that took over once he realized he was so far from anyone's help. He wants to tell him of the clenching panic as he rushed back through the woods, uncertain that he would make it back to his brother's house. How he had waited in his truck with the heat on, his brother's locked door just yards away, until it was late and he'd already figured out that nobody'd be coming home tonight. From here, the warden cannot see. So he stands.

For a moment, a man steps out into the world. Where the pavement meets the earth. Where metal and glass succumb to water, to air. In that same moment, something steps forward from that world, the briar and scrub, the green scum of the water's face. Its anatomy a balance between majesty and farce. The one set of eyes meets the other set of eyes from across a grey distance and they lock. Each validating by seeing. Each negating by turning away.

What do you do?

HYACINTH & WAXWING

Robbie arrived early that morning, sore in back and stiff in shoulders with eyes itching red from the long night crossing through one flat state into another—chasing taillights and hypnotized by highway lines, the green glow of interstate signs apparating from the vacuous black—but his mom and pop were up and waiting when he pulled in beside his pop's '78 Scout, so rest of any kind was out. His mother stepped down off the stoop and crossed the driveway to greet him. Pop remained in the open front door, leaning on his cane. He was making a face that Robbie took from experience to be a smile despite how much it looked like a wince. In the driveway gravel, his mom hugged Robbie hello. It was familiar, her gesture, if not also formal.

It was a wet October grey outside, with just a few blue jays here and there in the gutters and defoliating trees, whinging like rusty hinges to mock the neighborhood's morning stillness. No one else roaming the cul-de-sac.

Few windows lit on the street. Robbie followed his parents inside the house, let himself be led to the kitchen, expecting to be greeted by the sour smell of medicine bottles and age but discovering only the ghost of last night's goulash lingering convivial in the air as they gathered around the red Formica table. Robbie fought the impulse to help his father ease into his seat, knowing already precisely how Pop would refuse him. He wasn't here to help his parents. He was here to be here. As vain as it felt to admit, he knew and accepted that his presence was his gift to them. He would be whatever they wanted him to be. And right now, they wanted him to be fed. His mom fixed him a cup of coffee then poured three bowls of bran flakes with honey drizzled over top. Then they crunched through breakfast as a team, pearls of milk dripping from their spoons. Just like when he was a kid.

His mom alone spoke while they ate. She kept talking when she cleared their empty bowls. But Robbie was having a hard time understanding her. Her voice had become like a songbird's, chirruping up into giddy high registers. It didn't seem to matter if he responded to her or not. Clearly, it was the talking itself that brought her joy. Watching her shuffle briskly about the kitchen, Robbie found himself thinking of her as a giant plum that, by nature's process, was slowly drying into a prune. Meanwhile, his pop was a pole bean, withered on the vine. Shaped so much like a question mark. He barely spoke one word. Over the shushing of her slippers, his mom's song seemed to indicate that she wanted him to go shopping with her. She was thinking new sheets and bedspreads and curtains for the spare bedrooms upstairs. There was also a new slots casino outside of town that she was curious to see. Robbie nodded and smiled and said sure. He wanted so much to sleep. Too bad. Fingering the wet circles left by his cup on the table's red face, Robbie looked over at his pop, whose fingers too were moving, tapping out rhythms against the crook of his cane held loosely between his knees. He was wearing plaid pajama bottoms and a red sweatshirt with an elephant and the word ALABAMA marching across the front. Neither article fit him terribly well. Staring at the black and white checks of his father's pajama bottoms, Robbie asked him, "Is there anything you need while we're out, Pop?" It was a foregone conclusion that his father would not be joining them on their outing.

Pop turned toward Robbie without really looking at him, broadening his smile that wasn't a smile. As if he was hiding behind his own face. His eyes through his glasses' blur were just thick hyphens.

"No thank you, Robek," he drawled, voice both mucousy and dry. "I don't need one thing today."

Jacek stood at the door and waited until Mala and his son had backed out of the driveway, Robek behind the wheel of his Scout, tires popping on the gravel and finally disappearing around the cul-de-sac's bend. He smiled and waved as he watched them go, but really, he was trying to keep his cane from shaking beneath his weight. Drive faster, he thought. Quit waving already and go. He shut the door and went to find his walker.

It was one of those things he didn't like anyone to see, his slow shuffle about the house with his four-legged metal brace dully cutting his path through the world, nudging chairs and knocking the wainscoting. There was some semblance of dignity with a cane. Not so with a walker. If a cane was a poem, a walker was a manual, read aloud and broadcast with a bullhorn. Jacek hated being seen so feeble.

In the hallway, somehow, one slipper fell off his foot. Jacek stopped to stare it down, as if it were a bad dog that might be convinced, by the sheer weight of his disappointment, into being a good dog. It didn't work. Disgusted, he left it behind in the search for his walker.

Being seen at all had, in recent years, become a thing the old man loathed. It felt like a violation. Growing old, he thought, should be private. Like masturbation, or using the toilet. Private. Measuring his steps to the kitchen, Jacek hung his cane over the back of his chair and withdrew his walker from behind the stove, snapping open its folding legs. Then he poured himself a glass of juice. Why should anyone want to bear witness to a body falling apart?

And did it gall him that Mala, two years his senior, could walk briskly about just fine, quick and nimble as a freshly hatched chick? Did it kill him that this spritely bird got to watch him crumple like a crushed cigarette? He finished his juice without realizing he was drinking. On the counter near the stove was a little black radio. Jacek clicked it on and a man's voice entered the room in midsentence, talking about a bill that would not pass through Congress. How can obvious things count as news? He turned off the radio and headed toward the bathroom.

Yes. Privacy. It's better when there's no one to see. In the hallway, he passed the traitorous slipper, pretending it wasn't there. Jacek knew that, at his age, he should be happy that Robek had come home for a visit, that the company of one's children was something that retired folk were supposed to revel in. But what's so great about being weak and defeated before the eyes of your son, simple boob that he may be? Isn't that the opposite of what any father would want? It was nice that Robek came, that he took the time to demonstrate the dimensions of his love. But a postcard would have sufficed.

Shuttling into the bathroom, Jacek clicked shut the door and surrendered himself coolly to the toilet's porcelain kiss. And finally, he could relax. Being observed by anyone but Mala made him self-conscious. His doctor made him self-conscious. Answering the phone made him self-conscious. But let it go. Jacek slouched on the toilet and told himself, let it go. You have grown old because you have grown. Your body betrayed you because it's a body. Maybe your son looks on you with pity and maybe he looks on you with love. Let him look. Let him eat your cereal and borrow your car. It changes nothing. He will be in this position, too, someday. All of these things are okay.

But still: sitting alone in the privacy of one's own bathroom? Positively luxurious. He remembered having to make his post-op movements in a hospital bedpan while Mala and a nurse looked on, and he remembered squatting in an Army latrine among a dozen other men. Why does no one ever tell you to appreciate this, the simple joy of a solitary shit? Maybe, he thought, I should write a song about it. Perhaps something in Bm.

Jacek began to hum a melody, something of the mountains and dark-haired girls and reminiscent of his youth, and maybe for a moment he imagined himself a younger man, the sort still capable of simple physical feats, such as standing while pulling up his pants in a single fluid gesture, for that is what he attempted in rising from the toilet. But his balance was bad and his legs got tangled in his pajamas as he pitched forward through the legs of his walker, which snapped closed on him as he landed hard and awkwardly on the floor, smacking his forehead on the corner of the sink on his way down. His glasses tumbled somewhere far away from his face. Everything was a blur, then the blur grew red from the gash blossoming on his brow. None of it hurt, but this knowledge did not comfort him, for only the inert feel no pain. It happened too quick, but none of it was a surprise. He was down. With his last bit of strength, Jacek tried to tug up the waistband of his pajamas to cover himself, and when he knew he could not, he said aloud or maybe just thought, like a kid's balloon whipped away in sudden wind, "What a load of crap."

They drove first to Filene's Basement on one side of the mall and then to JCPenney on the other side, then back again to Filene's to get the sheets and curtains his mom decided would look best in the upstairs rooms. "These frequencies," she said of the colors, "will heterodyne like *crazy!*" Then they took County Highway A through the open tracts of field and pasture past the outskirts of town, to the new slots casino to take a look around. It was nice driving his father's Scout. It felt less like an automobile and more like a wagon, something drawn by horses or an ox. You didn't so much drive it, he thought, as help guide it where it had already made up its mind to go. It didn't need him as much as he needed it.

They parked in a spot where there weren't many other

cars, then walked around through the casino in a slow, unguided daze like stoned teens overwhelmed at the fair. Neither had much interest in playing the machines. They just wanted to see what it was all about. The place was smaller than either Robbie or his mom had expected. Carpet like Navajo jewelry reinterpreted as a black velvet painting. Lots of flashing lights and dinging bells. Despite the sprawling parking lot outside, there was nearly no one playing the slots. Acting on a sense of obligation, his mother pumped a ten dollar bill into a quarter machine, pulled the lever a couple of times, and ended up with her ten dollars back in change. Then they found a sort of cafeteria buffet, stood in line and sat down with their trays, his mother trilling her birdsong all the while, and as they cut into their ham steaks and gravy, he heard her say something about oil drops bouncing on the surface of a magnetized superfluid and, in a moment of sudden dissociation, realized she was talking about quantum physics.

"This article," she said, "made it sound like such a big deal, a real breakthrough, that observable matter actually *does* behave the same way as subatomic particles." She jabbed a spear of green bean into the gravy welling in her mashed potato volcano. "But jeez, just look at a model of electrons spinning around a nucleus and tell me it doesn't look like the solar system. Big things and little things *always* behave the same. The universe isn't interested in size."

Robbie had taken just enough science in college to recognize that he had no idea what she was talking about.

"I mean, look at a line of trees blowing in the wind. Now tell me, how are those not eyelashes?"

"Wait. How do you know all this?"

But she just shushed him with a dismissive wave of her hand.

All his life, Robbie has thought of his parents as dumb. The way that all kids think their parents are dumb. His father with his accordion? His mother with her meetings each evening at the Y? Idiots. Every action he has ever taken toward them has been to humor them. But what if he was the one being humored? What if he was the joke?

I'm not a kid anymore, he thinks, sopping up the last of his gravy with a hank of buttered roll. I haven't been for some time. He pauses eating long enough to check his phone for nothing in particular. Where did Pop play all those years, back when he still could play? What were Mom's meetings all about? Standing from the table, he buses his and his mother's trays, comes back with paper saucers of pineapple upside-down cake crowned in spiraled turrets of whipped cream. Why am I only just now growing up?

Mala raps her fork three times against the table. She's

not looking at him. But she wants his attention.

"I mean, think about it. They keep looking at smaller and smaller things trying to figure out where it all ends, right, trying to find the smallest basic unit. But it's no different than the astronomers with their telescopes looking deeper and deeper into space and finding no limit whatsoever, just more and more stuff. Stars and galaxies and junk spinning real fast." She turns her cake a quarter turn, then a quarter turn again. Like she's looking for the best place to begin. "The more you look, the more you find."

Robbie nods, not listening, and takes his first bite of cake. He wonders: What makes me think I'm growing up now?

Okay, so there's matter, right? And then there is dark matter. There is dark energy, too. These dark parts explain gravity, apparently. They explain a lot of things we don't yet know how to prove. For example: the universe is moving too fast, it seems, faster than the mass of its matter would allow. So the dark matter makes up the difference. It does most of the work. In fact, it does nearly all of it. There's more dark matter in the universe than there is of the real stuff, and even more dark energy than that. But we can't see any of it. We only know (or are told) that it's there. We have faith in the dark that is invisible and is everywhere. All we can see is matter, and there's barely any of that at all. So how do we know it's there? If all we can see and record and touch is the universe manifest as its least aspect, how can we even know it's there? How can we know *we* are *here*? Could it be that we are mostly dark, too?

Mala turns her absent gaze from the window to the man guiding the Scout along the highway, and wonders if it matters if it's Robek or Jacek behind the wheel. Everything is dark and likely getting darker. She wonders if it's either. She wonders if it's both.

They take their time driving home. Mala wants to point out to him through the windows things that have changed since he moved away to, as she puts it, become a big-shot barista in the city. It's important that he sees how much even the simplest things change, how everything is impermanent. Everything but the rules. But again, he's having a hard time understanding her. He's too damn tired, and the overcast sky makes the plains look flat and shadowed so that far and near grow indistinct and are maybe nearly the same. It doesn't make sense to him, how every word she says sounds like it's spoken in some other language he's hopeless but to misunderstand, her meaning always—always—just beyond his means. His mother speaks like a waxwing.

Back home, Robbie takes the shopping bags to one of the spare rooms upstairs while his mom prepares a fresh pot of coffee. When he comes downstairs, he asks her where Pop is. He's looking down the hallway at the lone slipper on the floor when he asks. Mala says he's likely taking a nap, but in a moment she goes into their downstairs bedroom and returns shaking her head, saying no, he's not there after all. They look around for him, in the backyard and in the garage. It's Mala who finally checks the bathroom.

"Oh jeez."

"What? What is it?" Robbie's in the living room, looking dumbly at the empty couch.

"I found your father." Then, more quietly and mostly to herself, "Damnit, Jacek."

Robbie comes and stands beside her in the doorway.

"Oh."

"Yeah."

"Oh no."

"I know." She lays her fingers across her cheek, looking at the blood congealed darkly on the checkered linoleum. "I guess we should call someone, huh?"

"Should we maybe check him or—"

Mala turns to him and touches his elbow. She gives him a look that he's embarrassed to be given. "Honey," is all she says.

While Mala makes the call, Robbie paces a bit in the

living room, his course a triangle from the TV to the couch to the bookshelf running along the back wall. On top of the television stands a framed photograph he's never noticed before, of a golden retriever panting in green grass, sun flare streaming from above distant trees. As far as Robbie can recall, they never owned a dog. It's the only framed picture in the room.

Robbie goes back to his father in the bathroom. It's almost like a mousetrap, the way the walker snapped closed on his pop. He notices, the toilet seat is up. And on the edge of the sink: a tiny bit of skin. It smells bad in here. He leans over his father to flush the toilet and is horrified by what he sees inside.

"Jesus, Pop, who taught you how to shit?"

He pushes the lever and closes the lid. Then he tries to pull up his father's pajama bottoms. He doesn't want the police or EMTs or whoever is coming to see his pop so exposed. But it's harder than he expected. Pop's legs are perfectly tangled.

Mala steps into the doorway.

"What was that sound?"

"I flushed the toilet."

"What for?"

"I thought—There was—What do you mean, 'What for?'"

Mala closes her eyes and shakes her head. "Quit messing with your father and come out here already.

They'll be here soon."

They sit in the kitchen drinking coffee until the police and ambulance arrive. There are a lot of questions to answer then, though none of them seem that important. Robbie lets Mala do most of the talking. She has to spell out for the police his father's name—Jacek Wozniak—and then spell out her own, Mala Nadja Milosz, then explain how they were never married, which Robbie supposes he'd always known but somehow, in this circumstance, doesn't seem right. Or anyway, not fair. As if in death, they should be wed. But he's forgetting that this was their choice. No one forced them to remain legally distinct.

It's late when the ambulance and police finally leave. The last time Robbie sees his father, Jacek is strapped to a gurney and being led by a pair of EMTs out the door into the night. Like a regular living patient. But really, all Robbie sees is the sheet pulled over the body.

They mill around for a while downstairs, not speaking, after that. It feels to Robbie like they ought to call someone, to share the bad news. But who on earth could they possibly call? Eventually, Mala fills a basin with hot soapy water, and together they sponge the blood up off the bathroom floor. They wipe the blood from Jacek's walker, and fold it closed properly, and lean it in the corner. They clean the toilet and the sink and the bathtub while they're there, too, folding the piece of skin from the sink in a square of paper towel and throwing it in the trash.

They pour the bloody water from the basin into the toilet and flush, then wash the toilet again. Then they go upstairs and make the beds with the new sheets and bedspreads and hang the new curtains in the windows. The primary reds and blues look good against the stark white walls. When they're done, Robbie holds his mother for a while in the middle of his old bedroom, and her body feels so soft in his arms like there's some pillowy distance between them. He's not entirely certain who is comforting whom. Outside the windows, the blue jays are rolling their Rs. Throughout the house: no other sound than the quiet counter-rhythms of their breath.

Back downstairs, Robbie makes more coffee while Mala washes the juice glass Jacek left on the counter. They sit at the table with their steaming cups. Mala deals some cards, then scoops them up and deals again. Robbie stands and makes them each a bowl of bran flakes. He drizzles the honey slowly, watching how it catches the light. Mala shuffles and sings something at him and shuffles again. But he doesn't understand. They sit across from one another with Jacek's cane still hanging from the back of his chair, spoons clicking against bowls, and for the second time today—to the music of crunching and the sweet taste of honey melting into milk—at his parents' table, Robbie feels like a child.

GIRLS' SCHOOL

She does not remember how it began. The seed of the idea becoming a plan that becomes sneaking past her snoring roommate to quietly click closed the door at her back, to slip down the dormitory hall past rooms shut tight against the dreams of the girls inside. Low dim lights running the length of the hall just a few inches off the floor, pale will-o'-the-wisps, always remind her of a movie theater, or really a theater as seen in a movie, the creeping surreality of David Lynch. As if she is passing not through a place but a time where she should not be, the true dormitory revealed in the night as distinct from the false dormitory of the day. In the hidden company of something neither good nor evil but beyond either, watching unseen from the shadows. Like the dusky lounges of *Blue Velvet* or *Mulholland Drive*. She thinks of movies and thinks of David Lynch every time she walks on fox-soft steps past rooms of sleeping girls. It's as much a part of the ritual as anything else.

As one of the longest-term students at the girls' school—early admittance in eighth grade on scholarship for an essay on predetermination—she knows the secrets of the grounds:

She knows night alarms secure all the dormitory's exterior doors but none of its windows;

She knows the dorm is built into a hillside, so knows the window on the back stairwell's landing is only five feet off the ground;

She knows she can slip easily out and in: a mink or caracal;

She knows the way across the quadrangle even blind-folded by a new moon and knows which of the main school building's basement windows lock and which do not;

She knows, at this hour, the security guard is sleeping with a newspaper in his lap, slouching at his post by the front doors;

She knows she drifts unseen.

In through the unlockable basement window, dark ponytail swishing over shoulders and back, she takes her time crossing the dark cellar space. In its own way, with its warm mechanical hum and the cool touch of cement under bare feet, this place too calls to her. Secret and dark and, for this moment, hers alone. But this is an incidental place, a way station. A secret, but not *her* secret. Purposeful though unhurried, she passes through.

The basement mechanical room opens into a long hallway checkered in white-and-blue tiles catching the faint light leaking in from either end: stellar blue from the left, exit-sign red from the right. She knows in the red glow lies a set of stairs rising into the gymnasium. Wide echoing cathedral to sweat and yelling, bleachers folded, backboards cranked to the rafters. Its smell a reflection of its shape. But she does not walk toward the gymnasium.

She does not know how this started. In many ways, it's like a constant. Hidden behind the curtain of everything else.

The open cavern of the natatorium—like the mechanical room, like the swath of night between dorm and school—carries its own soft, deep hum. But its song is a different song. The purr of a kitten versus the purr of a lion. Not asleep. Just waiting. With the pool lights on, the water glows a warm and dream-like blue—the same blue, she thinks, as some ancient stars, cooling but still warm, still giving—flashing thirstily against pillar and tile. Above everything, a gigantic skylight the exact size and shape of the pool hangs suspended in the natatorium's ceiling. An unblinking eye staring up into the night. A lens of black reflecting a lens of light.

At the edge of the pool, she feels the natatorium's hum vibrating all around her. Feels it hum through her. The back of her legs. Her belly. The tender hollow behind each ear. Where her jaws click together. Where her lips meet.

Humming gently through. She steps out of her sweatpants and underwear, leaves her tank top on the floor, steps into the wet kiss of water. Warmer than her skin.

She does not remember the first time, she thinks, because every time is the first time. All times happen simultaneously. There is this, happening forever. Then there's everything else, outside. On her back, she floats out into the center of the pool, and this is her first time, and this is her every time. Because the natatorium is underground, its roof and skylight are level with the ground: in fall it skitters with nervous reds and yellows, in winter it snakes with veins of snow, spider webs of frost, but tonight it is April and spring-clear and she can see the milky spray of stars repeating and expanding farther than she can understand. And that's okay. Not understanding is okay. With her ears below the water, she hears the natatorium's hum so much clearer. Surrounding her. Singing through. The water a buoyant light holding her up, a thousand tiny tongues or maybe one enormous tongue moving with and within her. The soft line of her neck. Her lower back and the swell of her hips. The cleft of her sex. Her calves and her knees. Her whole body suspended and caressed by a singular, considerate tongue of light. A million tongues. One tongue.

She does not remember when this began. This has always been. The truth behind the cloud of everything else she has ever seen or done. Going to school a cloud.

Laughing with friends a cloud. Her parents and home and watching movies each a cloud. Behind everything else, there is this, always this, shining blue through her body into the night sky above. This is where she's always been. She will always be here. She will always be here. She will always be here.

BUTTERSCOTCH

The tires spat dust and pebbles at me as my wife pulled our car off the shoulder onto the dirt road. I stood and watched her disappear, red taillights winking out behind the leafless trees. Then I stood there a while more. It wasn't late yet but was getting dark anyway, the sky all milky orange and deep blues. It reminded me of something, but I couldn't remember what. I had on my favorite brown corduroy suit, the one I call my funeral suit. It was approaching the first night in November. It wasn't cold yet, but it'd be here soon. I started walking.

I could have turned back toward home but decided to keep going the way we'd been driving before my wife stopped to kick me out. I had no intention of going to the party now, but there was more than just the party in the direction we'd been headed. And anyway, I already knew what home was about. The road curved slowly to the left and up a hill covered in dense hickory and oak. To my right, an old wall of collapsed fieldstone followed the road among a windbreak of witchy beech. A long meadow stretched out beyond that, reaching toward where the sky lapped with color and the sun wanted to set. I didn't know Connecticut could look like this until I moved here. Now I forget it can look like anything else.

Maybe a half-mile passed and I didn't see any houses, but soon I heard the slow approach of a car and in a dark spot among the trees, an Oldsmobile crept to a stop alongside me. It was heading the same direction that my wife had gone. A young man and woman were inside. The car was a boat. It was burgundy. But that might have just been the light. The woman rolled down her window and the man leaned across the console to get a better look at me—I remember, he propped his elbow in between the woman's knees—then asked if I needed a ride. From somewhere far away came the diffuse sound of a cow moaning in a field. All three of us looked to where we thought the moan came from. I shrugged and said okay.

The backseat was piled up in pumpkins. I had to stack them on one side so that I'd have a place to sit. They were all the same milky orange color as the sky. But the sky didn't look like that anymore. To head off his question, I asked the man driving which way they were going, and the woman said they were just going for a drive. She was wearing a navy dress with red lilies printed on the fabric. He was wearing a dark jacket. I couldn't see if he had on a tie. I told them a drive sounded perfect. The woman turned and smiled at me. The man put the Olds in gear.

What the man was doing, in a technical sense, was driving, but really what he was doing was idling. The car drifted slow as a phantom up the wooden dirt road, the world revealing itself at nearly the same unhurried pace as when I'd been walking. I rolled down the window and felt the cool sweet air pour softly over me. The man said something I couldn't hear to the woman, and she laughed.

Through the windows we could watch the drama of squirrels and chipmunks blitzing through fallen leaves, hunting out acorns or beechnuts for their larder. It reminded me of a time when I was younger and my friend and I caught a chipmunk. We'd driven off into the woods and were goofing around when we saw it zipping around. There was something about its movements that seemed too professional. It was all business. It wasn't anything, in our current state of mind, that we could abide. We chased it around the understory amid the leaning trees, and when my friend flushed it out from beneath a bush, I bent and scooped it up in my hands. It didn't resist much after that. We took it back to the pickup and set it on the bench seat and fed it peanuts out of a can and the animal was immediately tamed. It let us pet it and scratch between its ears. I remember, it made a sound like it was purring. It really wasn't much different than a hamster. We drank beer and played with the chipmunk, then eventually set it free, though later I found a couple wood ticks buried in the soft parts of my hands. I wanted to tell this to the man and woman I was riding with, but I suspected they wouldn't believe me.

At the crest of the hill, the trees fell away for an old white farmhouse where a woman was taking down her clothes from the line. She looked tired. A gigantic hex mark loomed above the barn doors. On the down-slope of the hill ran a pasture full of black cows, and when we saw them we each pointed, then laughed. We were all thinking the same thing. The best jokes are the ones no one has to say. After the pasture was a windbreak and in the valley another farm began. In our idling drift, we could see a man walking from the farm through the fields near us, leading a tiny pony. He didn't have a hold of any halter or rein. The pony simply followed him. It walked funny. The man led the pony to a dark spot in the fields and when we were parallel with them on the road, the young man driving stopped the car. We sat and watched the farmer stroking the pony's head and ears. He scratched between its eyes. It looked like he fed it a sugar cube. Then he pulled a pistol out from his pocket and shot the pony in the head.

The sound of the gun took a long time to fade out through the valley. The pony fell into the dark spot, so now it was just a man standing near a black patch in a field. We waited a second, then all of us got out of the car. I stepped on the wire fence so the man and woman could cross over. We walked the field toward the farmer. The grass just barely held frost.

We'd almost reached the farmer before he saw us. He'd had his head down. In one hand he held a dirty white rag and in the other he held the gun. He was using the rag to wipe the gun clean. In the low light, the white rag softly glowed. At his feet there was a hole in the ground and in the hole lay the pony. He must have dug the grave in advance. When he saw us coming, he stopped cleaning the gun. The pistol rested in the rag.

"Her legs were sick," he said. "She'd get down on the ground and scrape them all around in the dirt. She'd do that 'til she was bloody. Just tear herself apart. I think something itched in her bones." I looked down into the hole, but I couldn't see where the bullet split the pony's head. It did not look asleep. "What are you supposed to do about that?" The farmer dropped his head again and seemed startled to see the gun in his hand, like he forgot he'd been holding it. He wrapped the white rag around the pistol and put them both back into his pocket. So now his hands were empty.

We stayed and helped bury the pony. We each took a turn with the shovel. There was a pile of dirt near the hole. I'd missed that before. I didn't like when we had to toss dirt on the pony's face. But you can't half-bury a horse. You have to bury the whole thing. Even the pretty parts.

When we were done, the farmer shook our hands.

Then he reached in his coat pocket and handed us some hard candy. He had to take the gun out of his pocket to do this. The pistol was blocking the candy. It's what he'd fed the pony before shooting it. Not sugar cubes. Butterscotch. I guess it was left over from Halloween. We each took a candy and unwrapped the yellow wrapper and put the candy in our mouths, and I remember, the taste was stronger than I'd expected. Sweeter. We smiled at the farmer and he smiled back but it was clear he didn't mean it. He nodded and walked back toward his farm. It was the slowest walk I'd ever seen.

Back in the car, the young man started the engine and put on some music. We all felt sad after the whole deal with the pony. He wanted us to feel better. He found some kind of doo-wop on the radio and in a moment, the girl was bopping along in her seat. Then she sang. She knew all the words, even though the song was old—older than me—and even knew the different harmonies. She was terrible. Then the man joined in. He was terrible, too. The road ended at an intersection with a gas station where the county highway ran through, and I expected him to turn toward town, but instead he went the other way. Then he turned down a road I didn't know. When the song ended, they both laughed, and before the next song started, I asked what they planned to do with all these pumpkins. The woman turned to face me with a confused look on her face, like she'd never heard the word before. Pumpkin.

In the rearview mirror, the man caught my eye and said, "What pumpkins?" But I could tell from his eyes: he was smiling.

It was nighttime outside now. The music was quieter and I could hear the road passing underneath. Sometimes, through the trees, I could see the light of a house. Again, I wanted to tell them about my friend and the chipmunk, but before I could, the woman turned around in her seat and said to me that she was glad they'd picked me up. She said I was fun, and the man agreed. I didn't know what to say to that, so I tapped out a beat with my fingers on a pumpkin. It sounded good, so I did it some more. Like a little Indian drum. They laughed. I held a pumpkin under my arm and really went to town. Then without much warning, the man pulled the car up to a house I'd never seen before, where the lights all shined like butterscotch in the windows and cars were parked haphazardly through the yard. There was music. Through the windows, I could see shadows move. But in one window, a shadow stopped and did not move again. The soft black shape of a woman, watching. The man turned off the engine and without saying anything he and the woman got out, so I got out, too, still playing a little pumpkin like a drum. My new friends hurried hand-in-hand toward the bright and lighted house that belonged to someone I did not know. I followed them, but then I stopped. Indistinct voices and the smell of dead leaves. The night's deepening shroud and the cool pumpkin in my hands. Everything grown fuzzy at the edges. The shadow woman in the window was gone. I stood still and stared with the taste of hard candy still haunting the flesh of my mouth, before this strange house, among all these strangers' parked cars, and I thought I saw, though I could not be sure, the one I owned with my wife.

TROCHA STEP

She rides up to him on a tall white horse, its stark hide a bell striking the copper of her skin. Its gait is slow because it is her will, and she is smiling. Her body is what she's been trying to say.

With stray-dog patience, he watches. She draws closer, but he doesn't believe she'll ever get there. Even when she does. Hoof-marks scratched in dust. He takes the cigarette from his lips. Then he puts it back. "Get off my horse," is what he says in between.

A FLUENT BLUE

A boy with a rowboat articulates his summer by ferrying tourists between two islands. From Monhegan's sandy beach bound by towering cliffs to the high grassy knuckle of Manana. Sculling over blue-green waves, he makes a fast five bucks each trip. And too, it's fun for him: what boy does not dream of captaining his own little ship at sea?

There is no uniformity to the tourists he ferries over. Some are solo, often men who grew up here on this toothy coast whose lives have dictated they move somewhere far from home. Those are the quiet trips. There are families from distant cities, giddy and agog at the simple act of crossing above water in a paint-peeling wooden skiff. There are anxious young couples, eager to be alone on an unpeopled island. The boy takes them all.

One family in particular, the boy remembers. A mother and father and very young daughter. Dressed too nice to be locals. Their accent an absence of accent. The family's plan is to take a leisurely walk through the high grassy dome of Manana while the boy waits for them by the slip, stretched out in the boat's belly and reading a book on mice. Everyone agrees: this is a good plan. Through the crossing, the mother is quiet and also looks tired, as if their vacation contains some built-in strain. The daughter is two maybe and mews like a cat: the indistinct sounds of an animal contented. The father, meanwhile, is a babbling cartoon, narrating their brief passage through the harbor like it's a sporting event, like a great moment in history. He shouts and gesticulates. He mistakes every buoy for a loon. For the boy, the crossing is the longest fifteen minutes of his life. For the mother, it likely feels longer.

What's clear is this: throughout his own childhood, the father spent his summers on Monhegan. Running kites along the high cliffs. Watching for seals in the harbor. They've become a kind of dream-like jewel, his memories of Monhegan summers. And now he can share that jewel with his wife, with his daughter. This is his first return to the islands as an adult. His excitement boils over, over boils.

The boy does his best to suffer the man's exuberance in silence. It's obnoxious, he thinks, to so blatantly be a tourist, a summer person, a visitor. He has not quite realized: his relationship to this place might very well someday be identical to the man's.

From her pocket, the mother produces a hank of cloth,

lightly dabs the sweat from her own and her daughter's face. The boy can tell: this kerchief was once part of a dress. Her husband points at a seagull and coos.

To distract himself from the sound and gestures of the father's unending monologue, the boy falls into meditating on the simple perfection of his old skiff's groaning oarlocks. There's the beauty of the object, sure, its gentle swoops almost like a horseshoe, both hard and masculine as a grappling fist yet elegant as the bell of a woman's swinging hips. But there is also the pure utility of the thing: every aspect of its design is to accomplish a task and accomplish it well. Its beauty a byproduct of its specialization. No ornament needed. It is perfect.

It's likely because of this adoring meditation that the boy loses one oarlock overboard. His attention is not on his task. Drawing the skiff alongside Manana's slip—at low tide, just a long ramp bearded in sea-moss and long ribbons of kelp—the boy raises the oars to stow beneath the bench seats, hears the splash of the popped-free lock, and too late knows exactly what he's lost.

An oarlock is designed to do one job well. Without it, that job is impossible.

The family, oblivious, clambers out onto the slip. The boy looks over the boat's flaking lip into the water's fluent blue. It's only maybe three feet deep here. But he cannot see bottom. So he cannot see the lock.

The boy knows he has time before he'll officially have

stranded them out on Manana. While the family takes its long walk through the grass, he can dunk into the water, grasp at the sandy bottom, seek out what he has lost. But what if he cannot find the lock on his own? What if the family helps him? What if he asks them for help? The child, being a child, is both peripheral to and at the center of the problem—unable to assist, her presence raises the stakes—but what if the father finds the oarlock, redeeming his previous obnoxious behavior by becoming the hero of the day? What if it's the mother, tired, harried, the first-time visitor proving her dominion over this place?

What if no one finds it?

The boy looks from the disguising water to the family on the slip, reveals—in his posture, in his eyes—his embarrassment and danger and need. Up the slip, the upward tide lips. The family validates him by looking back.

If each moment is discrete and unrepeatable—is, by accomplishing itself just the one way, only ever meant to be that one way—does that mean each moment is perfect? Its form indistinguishable from its function. Executing its one job well.

If your job is to find: what do you find?

Four people row to an island, each seeking one thing but arriving at something else.

AFTER THE INTROMIT

It's a grey and wet dawn ripe with silence and finches in which Cuth awakes slumped over the leather grips of his car's sweat-stained steering wheel. His head is pillowed against his arms and his car is pillowed against a bank of soft brush and leading backward from the car is the path it cut through the dead grass and weeds. Away from the dirt scratch of road. Barely missing a tall oak tree. The little birds gather on his hood and watch him through the windshield. Heads cocked. Eyes like oil. Tongue-fuzzy and slightly dizzy, Cuth gets out of the car to inspect the scenario, the cuffs of his pants soaking up the cold spring dew. It's almost gentle how the bumper nestles in among the bushes. The oak, only just beginning to bud out with new growth, stands like something delphic and forgotten. The car came within inches of its trunk.

"Stupid." To the sagging wet grass. To the flocking silent birds. "Totally dumb." He shouldn't have closed his eyes, shouldn't have trusted his own aim or the universe or its mandates. Defying the laws of entropy: who decided that he'd be the exception to the rule? Slouching back to his car, Cuth starts the engine without a hitch, backs out of the brush and onto the road, sets off thinking maybe he'll find another tree to run into or maybe a steep hillside to drive off. Instead, he goes to his sister's house.

It's a thirty-minute drive to Catherine's, over cracked county roads and roads of packed, rutted gravel. Early green fields and fields freshly turned, a deep hazardous brown. Lots of hills. Cuth makes the trip longer by pulling over to piss in a culvert, then again to chase some cows off the road. Once, as he's passing a sterling white farmhouse, a dog takes to running after his car, jetting from its yard and into the road, and Cuth taunts it by gradually slowing, creating the illusion that it might catch him before he accelerates and dwindles down the road and is gone. In this way, when he arrives, it is not to a sleeping house.

As it is, Catherine is in the dooryard when he pulls up, a wicker laundry basket balanced on her hip as she heads toward the clothesline and Ashley, too, is there, perched on the seat of her pink tricycle and dressed in purple sweats and helmet, riding circles in the yard. She breaks orbit when Cuth steps out of the car, pedals clacking and squealing and she squealing as well, calling his name as she races toward him, and before he knows to defend himself, the handles of her tricycle bark madly against his shin.

"Dear god fuck!"

"Uncle Cuth!"

She's off the trike and hugging him as he crouches, clutching his leg. She has no idea that he's hurt.

"Cuthbert?" His sister sets down her laundry, slowly approaches. "I didn't expect to see you today."

The wind moves her hair in an earthen sash over her right shoulder.

"Hi."

Snaps her dress like a flag.

"Or at all."

A banner above the ramparts.

"I thought I'd visit."

"It's early."

"Yep."

"What happened to your hair?"

None of his hair is left.

"It's gone, Cath." Across his skull, stubbled blue continents eroding into his scalp's pale sea. "All gone."

"Are you hurt or something?"

There's blood on his hands, in a spot on his shin. The little shit got him good. "I'm fine." Cuth wipes his hands clean in the cool wet grass, then picks up Ashley and joins Catherine at the clothesline. Helps his sister hang the wet clothes. Feels the dewy morning breeze cut through his shirt, through his bald skull, cool but soothing. Like the wet laundry in his hands. Like his sister's gaze. When the clothes are hung and the basket's empty, they head indoors for breakfast.

Inside is warm and wooden, dark wainscoting and exposed post and beam. Old timbers oiled almost black. Like someplace from the northern frontier. Forgotten territory. Which, in a sense, he supposes this is. Cuth always wants to believe that this is where he and his sister grew up. Measuring each other on a doorframe. Storing preserves and potatoes in the root cellar. Banking the house with hay bales for the winter. Their mother raised them in a third floor apartment above some coastal downtown. Yet still, each time he's here, he makes the same mistake. He looks for the pencil marks in the doorways. He remembers things that never occurred.

Catherine waits until her brother is held captive by coffee and pancakes washed in stewed fruit and syrup. Then the interrogation begins.

"So are you working yet?"

"Nope."

"Any intentions to?"

"Don't need to." He's referring to the settlement.

"Doesn't that get tiresome, living off someone else's money?"

Cuth points to the corners of the room with his fork's sticky tines, as if to indicate something that isn't there.

"I'm guessing John is still at work? Pulling the third shift now or something?"

John is Ashley's dad. From across the table, Catherine flips him off.

"How about women, do you not need those anymore either?"

"Jesus, Cath."

At the end of the table, Ashley—mercifully—tips over her plate, syrupy pancakes oozing onto the floor. Catherine scoots over to clean it up and soothe her crying daughter, to fix her a new plate, and Cuth takes advantage of the reprieve, finishes his breakfast in peace.

Later, while helping with the dishes, Cuth feels more than sees his sister come up behind him at the sink. Beneath the sudsy water, there are knives and also spoons. His hands are down there with them.

"Don't think," she whispers, her playfulness itself a sort of threat, "that I'm even close to being done with you."

Then again, for a little while, it seems like she might be. Cuth wonders why he invites this upon himself, the critical eye and tongue of his sister. What good could this possibly do him? Bellies full, he and Ashley go back outside so that she can ride circles on her tricycle, little tires scratching and biting at the driveway dirt. The world is on the cusp of thawing and freezing, not certain on which side of the line it wants to be, at any moment ready to change its mind. Cuth can't tell if he wants his sweatshirt on or off. He backs his car to the head of the driveway so that Ashley has more room to play. Inside the house, Catherine sweeps the floors and wipes the counters, enjoys a cup of coffee in silence, alone, watching her brother and daughter play through a speck-spotted window in the kitchen, unmoved and unseeing.

Eventually Ashley wants to ride her tricycle in the road—she is only four and though has at long last come to understand the meaning of "no," still chooses sometimes not to believe in it—so they have to put her ride away and play inside. The warmth of the kitchen stings their cheeks, draws a fleecy curtain through their minds, and together they laugh in surprised, uncomprehending bursts. Wordless, Catherine takes the phone out to the yard and calls a girlfriend. Cuth and Ashley watch her go, mouths open, then dump a crate of Legos across the living room floor.

Some games, Cuth is sure, define gender lines. Others defy. Who is not guilty of constructing one's own worlds? He and Ashley build a castle of primary colors. Yellows and reds. A tower for a princess and a turreted wall for the king. In the back, Cuth constructs a gallows. He does not tell Ashley what it is. While they build, Ashley launches into a story about a girl whom no one likes even though she is beautiful or maybe because she is beautiful, and so she's forced to do hard work or is maybe forced to run away, into the dark wilderness of a forest or cave. It's hard for Cuth to follow. Eventually he realizes that Ashley is describing to him a movie, a cartoon, one that she has not actually seen. But she loves this beautiful persecuted girl. Cuth's never been more certain of anything. Setting down a jumble of interlocking blocks, Ashley crawls over to nestle against her uncle's chest and asks with eyes cast down and voice suddenly crestfallen if he'd take her to the movie, and though neither knows its name or if any theater even shows it anymore, if any ever have, Cuth tells her that he'd love to. Which is not a lie.

After a moment, on the floor beside their tower and gallows, they each fall into a late morning nap. Inside the house, there are bats in the crawlspace attic and mice in the crawlspace cellar, mice and voles in the fields and fescue meadows outside above which circle hawks—black-eyed and red-tailed—and between each, in the gravel of her driveway, Catherine quietly weeps into the phone.

It's late morning, almost noon, when Catherine comes in and wakes them and though it is now clear to Cuth that something's wrong—that he has actually shown up in the middle of some crisis or other—she doesn't want to talk about it and he doesn't want to force the point. Outside, the day is getting no brighter, might even be darkening. The three pile onto the couch in the unlit living room, hide themselves under a thick down comforter, watch a science program about sharks.

For a while again, Cuth sleeps—it's becoming clear to him just how hungover he really is—and when he wakes, the program is over and Ashley is poking at the rope burn on his neck. Catherine's gone. A dark sound, steady but tremulous, moves about somewhere in the kitchen. When asked, Cuth tells Ashley it's a birthmark.

By lunch the sky has taken on a stormy sort of bruise, deep and purple. Catherine makes grilled cheese sandwiches and warms a can of tomato soup while Cuth and Ashley sit together at the table, engaged in a tournament of tic-tac-toe, drawing their decisive Xs and Os with fat orange markers on a big sheet of blue construction paper.

Once Ashley becomes occupied with shredding her sandwich and drowning the chunks in her soup with a spoon, Catherine resumes:

"So what're you doing out here, Cuth?"

"What do you mean?"

"Why'd you drive all the way out here? It's, like, four

hours from the city."

"It's three hours. I came to visit you guys."

"False."

"Well."

Outside, a gust of wind snaps the clothes on the line. Cuth wants to tell his sister about trying to hit the tree. About his attempt this winter to slide naked under the ice-sheet encasing a frozen tidal creek. About the noose that's been hanging from a rafter in his house for months. He wants to tell her the absurd joke of his life constantly being trumped by the repeated punch line of his failed deaths. Beside him, Ashley makes a roaring sound and gobbles up a cheesy bite.

"I'm trying, Cath. Why wouldn't I want to try?"

But what sort of response was he hoping for? Across the table from him, Catherine shrugs, stirs her soup, says nothing. And it occurs to Cuth that maybe even his sister is finally giving up on him, too. After all the reasons and evidence he's presented. She finally gets it.

They finish lunch and clean up the kitchen while from where she colors at the table, Ashley sings the unending song describing their movements around the room, interrupted now and then with images of horses and castles and princesses in towers, and all at once, John is home. No one even hears his truck pull in. He is standing by the kitchen door in overalls and a dirty white shirt, tall and lean and grinning like he's got this whole affair of life figured out and everyone else is a dink for not knowing too. Ashley slips from her chair and runs to tackle her father's legs, and John gestures to where brother and sister are hugging by the stove.

"Well ain't this fucking precious, huh?"

Cuth squints at his brother-in-law, trying to decipher something vague and unpleasant. A scent maybe. Possibly septic. Catherine had been putting water on for tea and in a sudden clear and unconfused urge, he wanted to hold her. It seemed like something anyone could see was needed, something anyone would want. Cuth stepped forward and touched her and she turned in to his embrace, holding on to his shoulders and hiding her face where his hair used to curl around his neck, breathing long and hard against the fabric of his shirt before John's voice trapped the breath in her throat. Slowly, in unison, they each drop their arms and step away.

John laughs once, a sort of inward confirmation, and bends to pick up his daughter. Crossing the kitchen to his wife, he pauses just long enough to run a finger up Cuth's throat, from clavicle to chin.

"Nice rope burn, chief."

The look Catherine shoots him makes Cuth feel shameful as a worm. The sort that lives in shit. But before anything more can come of it, John is beside her and raising her chin for a kiss, and again the room's attention is refocused.

"Oh, I'm just razzing him," he tells her.

"Where've you been?"

"Ha! Now that's the fucking question, now ain't it?" John sets down Ashley and opens the fridge, leans in, emerges with a can of beer. "But ain't that always the question."

It's like they're captives, the way Cuth and Catherine stand still while John moves freely about the room, pulling a chair away from the table and arranging himself in an easy, wide-legged pose, each knee pointed at a sibling. He drinks long and thirstily from the can and sets it on the table, helps Ashley clamber into his lap.

"Nice park job, by the way."

Cuth glances out the window, already spotted with the first drops of rain. His car is still parked near the road, blocking the whole driveway, fenders scratched from the brush he struck in the night. The grass is bent down where John drove his truck around and over the lawn.

"You out playing bumper cars in the woods or something?"

Cuth starts to answer or apologize or something but John waves him off. Catherine is giving him that look again, equal parts hurt and anger or maybe simply anger at being hurt, but when she speaks, it's to her husband.

"So are you going to tell us where you've been all this

time?"

John smiles and nods to himself, takes another long drink. In his lap, Ashley is playing with the buttons of his overalls, unhooking and reattaching the straps, unhooking and reattaching.

"Believe it or not, I've been stuck in traffic."

It's obvious that she doesn't—her body a rigid exclamation point, the end of a sentence tense and unspoken—but John nods and says yes to himself and continues.

"I was coming back from town along the Old Settlement Road, and I'm about halfway down when suddenly traffic's all backed up." Scratches his chin, laughs quietly to himself. "Of course, when I say traffic I mean myself and four or five other trucks and ahead of all that a tractor with a tiller that one of Hal Hancock's boys was driving from one field to another. But ahead of all that, and I can see this pretty clearly, are about eight or ten cop cars and a couple ambulances surrounding the old Jasper place."

It's at this point in the story that the kitchen becomes a blue painting behind frosted glass. John's voice comes muffled from beyond the canvas and paint.

"So I sit there for a while, you know, in no real hurry. I worked late or early as it were, then had coffee with the boys down at the Black Duck, and more than anything else, I'm spent. Too tired to care. But, you know, after fifteen, twenty minutes of just sitting there with other cars lining up behind you, well, a man gets curious."

The room is an echo of itself. Cuth can tell how this story ends.

"So I get out the truck and walk down to where all the law is gathered and even though we all know they ain't supposed to say squat, we also all know that we're all bound to figure this thing out one way or another anyway and besides, Lieutenant Pelkey there is my cousin Danny, so you know it's really not a secret at all what's happened. Shit, I could've figured it out myself just by looking. Blood and broken glass everywhere. The yellow tape fencing in a couple sheets in the driveway. The fact that it's the fucking Jaspers we're talking about here."

"John, please."

"I mean, the Hendersons or Duffs could have had an accident, right? But the fucking Jaspers? Those junky fucks?"

"John—"

"Of course Glen's gonna pop Becky one of these days. Course he's gonna finish the job on himself."

"John, Ashley is right there in your lap, goddamnit." Catherine is shaking, furious.

Stroking his daughter's hair, John watches her solemnly play with the snaps of his overalls, then chuckles. "Where are my manners? Honey, go play in your room for a spell, okay? We've got some big kid business to discuss in here."

Quietly, Ashley slips out of his lap and pads up the stairs. Cuth leans against the refrigerator and slides to the floor.

"So anyway," clearing his throat, "according to Cousin Danny, these two miserable fucks were getting right lit up as usual and one thing led to another and they got to arguing and I don't know, maybe Glen Jasper figured out that Becky'd been fucking every clown and handjob that ever wandered through this town, I don't know, but it looks like he dragged her out in the driveway by her hair and blew her brains out all into the dirt, then figured what the fuck and did the same to himself."

It's like the slow collision of one ship into another, the way John—grinning—turns to meet Cuth's eyes. "If I'm not mistaken, they were friends of yours, huh Cuthbert?"

Cuth nods. "Yes they were."

"Friends from way back."

"Yes they were."

"Fascinating shit."

Cuth doesn't tell them that he was at the Jaspers' last night. Sitting at their table. Drinking their gin while the couple smoked amazing amounts of hash. Glen shaggy and wild-looking and already mostly grey, telling jokes and being goofy. Knocking things over with his big dense beard. Sometimes burning his mustache on a hit. Frequently touching Becky's hand or cheek, her long blond hair, always fixing a fresh drink for her whenever she needed it, always hanging off every last one of her cigarette-contralto words. They drank through the night, the three of them, and Becky told them of the time she got stranded in France as a teenager without a word of French in her head and had to pantomime her way to the Italian border where she was able to catch up with her friends once again. They listened like warriors gathered around a fire. Memorizing the details. Parsing the meaning to again later pass on. At some point Cuth collapsed asleep in a guest room—the house was enormous, had been Glen's grandmother's before she died of emphysema—and in the night he awoke to a sound and found that their cat had birthed a litter of kittens in the pooled mess of his jacket on the floor, had given birth and now—more than anything else in the world—wanted to curl up in Cuth's lap, nestle her bloody body against him. He said no. He got up and dressed and left his jacket for the new family's nest, and when he left the house there were no dead bodies splayed in the driveway. Glen and Becky were a tangle of limbs on the living room couch, matching snore for drunken snore, and the sight of them filled Cuth with something troubled and indistinct. He watched them breathe for a long time. Then he took his car out into the night to crash it and himself into a tree.

But Cuth says none of this. Nodding, John repeats, "Fascinating shit."

In her corner of the kitchen, Catherine stands with her eyes down, lips folded tightly into her mouth. Then she speaks.

"So you worked late."

"Yeah."

"Then had breakfast at the Black Duck with some guys."

"Yeah."

"Maybe had a drink or two."

"Sure."

"Then this murder held you up."

"Catherine."

"All of which takes you, what, seven hours?"

"Catherine."

"Seven hours to eat breakfast and take the long way home."

"It's a long fucking way to have to backtrack, Catherine."

It gets worse from here. It's happening in a space beyond what Cuth can hear. He sees Glen and Becky tangled together on the couch. He sees them sprawled dead at the feet of cops. Still tangled. Matching one for one. Standing, he tells Catherine and John that he's taking Ashley to the movies—if they even hear him, they must be relieved: to have the house empty, to be free to rip one another to shreds in private—sways upstairs to Ashley's room, helps her get dressed and out the door and into his car.

The rain has finally agreed to come down and come down hard. Roaring against the roof. Washing out and reshaping the road. Buckled into the passenger seat, Ashley makes up a song, rocking her head from side to side and outpouring one long sinuous verse about towers and sunlight and the pretty girl that no one likes. Cuth wonders if the pretty girl is a brat, or one of those caustic beauties, the sort that everyone wants to adore but is forced by her actions to loath. He wonders about his niece's obsession with this cartoon girl. He wonders about a lot. As Ashley sings and he drives through the storm at a rate he knows is much too fast, Cuth's mind wanders a vague associative path and he is lost, stumbling down the blind alleys of his memory, and when he passes the old sterling farmhouse something black lurches before him in the road and he curses, shouts and jerks the wheel to the right, then to the left but he's sliding in the mud, tires dragging horribly as the car pitches right like a man with a bad limp and all at once they're stopped and in a ditch.

"That fucking dog!"

Beside him, Ashley is wide-eyed and surprised, silent. Through the crash, she didn't make a sound. Cuth stares at his niece for a while. Gathers in her safety. Gathers in her shock. He breathes like he's thirsty even after a long drink. He pounds on the wheel and kicks the floor.

"Fuck fucking that goddamned fucking mutt!"

But this, he knows, is probably worse. So he stops. Closes his eyes and leans back into the seat. Listens to the rain wash over the car. Listens to the engine's quiet rumble, still running. Without opening his eyes, he turns off the ignition. And waits. And waits.

"I'm sorry, Ashley."

"It's okay."

"No. It's not."

"Oh."

"Are you alright?"

"I think so."

"Me too."

"Okay."

"I'm really sorry."

"Okay."

"I'm going to walk to that farmhouse back there. I'm going to go call for help. My cell phone won't work out here. I need to go call for help. Will you be okay here by yourself for a few minutes?"

"Okay."

"Okay?"

"Okay."

Cuth steps out of the car, is immediately soaked. The passenger-side tires are completely lost in the muck and swelling runoff from the road. He needs a tow. His shin hurts amazingly now, like maybe he's struck it again somehow in the crash. In the ditch, where the town has come through to cut back the brush and left it to rot, Cuth finds a long length of branch and uses it as a crutch, drags himself up the slick embankment and onto the road. Starts walking toward the farmhouse. He can see his tire tracks cutting through the mud, how his car had slid for fifteen yards or more before succumbing to the ditch, and when he's halfway between the house and his car, he sees it. Huge and black and galloping through the rain. Mouth open and tongue lolling. Eyes inscrutable. Galloping straight for him.

"Go home, dog!"

Then:

"You fucking dog, go home!"

Then he's just screaming at it, roaring in some forgotten primitive language as the black and heaving body comes upon him and not even realizing what's happening, Cuth raises his stick two-handed like an axe, over his head and then straight down and the dog collapses and slides to a stop in the muck. Cuth stands and watches it, can see the bright patch of red opening from its black head, can see beyond its crumpled bulk his car and niece in the ditch.

He brings the stick down one more time.

Behind him, in the farmhouse, a downstairs light comes on.

Setting the stick down, Cuth drags the dog out of the road. Strokes its teeth-bared snout. Stretches the peeled-back skin to close the open wound on its head. Picks up his stick and leans heavily against it as he hobbles toward the farmhouse. Up the porch steps and to the door. Doorbell or knocker? Doorbell or knocker? Cuth drops the knocker and waits there in the rain, soaked and beaten and lost to himself, waiting to ask these people whose dog he just killed to help him get back on the road.

PINK HORSES / TOUCHED & BLESSED

It wasn't the last day of school, but for all the seriousness anyone—the kids, our teachers—could honestly treat a thing, Christ, it might as well have been. It wasn't even worth pretending we couldn't already taste summer sweetly on our lips. We were all of us just waiting on the clock to run out, the last bell that'd signify it was really the last bell.

And it was hot out. And dry. Walking home that afternoon—no memory of French, no memory of pre-calc—I can still see the dust kicking up around my All Stars. Even when there was sidewalk to walk on. Even when the road was paved. The smell of dust and the scrape of my heels. My backpack made my back real sweaty so my shirt and my backpack both clung to my skin, and the sun made my head feel high and vapid even though I hadn't yet gotten high. I'm positive, everyone felt the same way. Sun-dumb and dreamy with dust rising from our shoes.

So I walked from school along the access road running parallel to Main Street, then along Highland running parallel to the old train tracks with nothing but a rangy copse of weed-woods in between, walked up the hill and down our short dirt road that, as far as I know, has never had a name, and at the road's end our house stood just a little ways set back near some trees. If we hadn't had our own driveway, I'd've figured that dirt road was our driveway. And maybe it was. Wild grass and goldenrod crackling around a pair of dirt ruts. I wonder what anyone else thought about that. If anyone thought about it at all.

Already, thinking back on it, I can feel that heat fifteen years or older scrubbing stupid again my brain. Our house back then was just a weathered grey box with a roof and some flowers bunched around the foundation, and my mom's chocolate brown AMC Eagle was parked in the driveway with its egg-crate nose pointed toward the road and the back door behind the driver's seat open, and when I walked from the dusty road across our lawn, I looked in that open door and saw my mom sprawled asleep on the leather bench seat. One arm tossed over her eyes. Her legs from the knees down inclining out the car, her white moccasined feet flat on the pebbly ground. She was wearing that linen A-line I liked so much. She was showing a lot of leg. It was nice seeing her asleep and so peacefully at that. But it also made me low. I guess no one wants to see their mom so exposed and vulnerable. No one wants their mom to sleep on anything but a bed.

Across from my mom's open door, parked in the grass in front of the house, an old wooden chair with its back broken off that we kept around as a stepstool stood squarely in the middle of the lawn. Resting on its foot-worn seat waited the brown discus of a chocolate cake.

I looked from the cake to my mom to the cake. I simultaneously got it but didn't get it. Sweat beaded a tickly track down my neck. But the house was slicing a bare edge of shade on where I stood, so that made my brain's workings easier. I thought about maybe waking up Mom, but I knew how she was when waking was a surprise. Like a cat in a grain sack. True wild and in a panic. I fixed Mom's A-line to cover her knees, then walked over to my cake in the grass.

The cake was built of two identical layers on a robin's-egg platter and I guessed was double chocolate, and over its face in Smurf-blue icing Mom had piped the words. *Happy Birthday.* Beneath that was a shape I couldn't possibly decipher. Some flowers? There were no candles. I appreciated that. I collapsed in the grass and took off my backpack, felt the faintest breeze wash real cool my sweaty back. Dragonflies in patrolling geometries snapped the air all around me. I opened my bag and took out my weed. There was still a good eighth of orange-hairy bud left in the sandwich baggie and also a decent roach, so I rolled a joint and put that in the baggie and the baggie in my shirt pocket, then smoked the roach down to a papery nothing right there beside my cake. The scent started off resinous then got fruity and ended loudly black, yet pungent as it was, I wasn't worried about Mom. Until the sun sank low across the fields, she was out.

I guess once the roach was cashed I could've gone inside, maybe played the N64 I had on loan from my cousin, wearing out my thumbs on the toggles waiting for Mom to wake up. But the idea of sniping Russians in *GoldenEye* really didn't appeal to me right then. And anyway, I had other plans. Blue dragonflies parting to make way, I left my backpack in the grass by my cake and headed for the north end of town. Out where the old train tracks crossed the last lengths of Main Street before it reverted again to numbered highway, there was a little park, just a grassy slope and field with a basketball court near the road. Fine as it was, almost no one ever hung out there. You could sit at the top of that slope with the old rails real near and look out over everything and no one cared that you were there or what you were up to. What was there not to love? The roach had me scorched and a little bit skittish, jaw clenched and short of breath, so instead of the road, I pushed through the weedy woods and followed the tracks to the park, counting the creosote-soaked ties as I walked, but always my mind wandered and I lost count before ten. Which felt stupid at the time. It makes sense to me now.

All I wanted to do was sit in the grass and get a little more high and watch. If I'd thought to bring my headphones, I'd've listened to my headphones, too. *Pretty Hate Machine* or *Undertow.* Simple wishes. I hadn't expected babies. But I've always been bad at telling what kids' ages are. Maybe they were toddlers. Whatever. Babies. I left the tracks to claim my spot on the slope right where I'd always intended to be, but there were the babies, two sexless, pudgy babies. And no one else! I looked. Maybe they were old enough to be out there on their own, I don't know. But I doubt it. They were old enough anyway to logroll down the slope, though, and know that that was fun. They were old enough to crawl back up and squeal and do it again. So I guess that meant everything was fine? I sat down in the grass a little ways off, and at the top of the slope near tumbling babies, I lit my joint, and I watched.

On the courts across the park from me, the boys were playing basketball. I could have set my watch by it if I wore a watch. Those boys were always on the courts, always playing ball. I was far enough away that I couldn't tell by looking who exactly was who. But I knew. There were eight of them, all from the varsity team, playing shirts versus skins and the four I liked best were the ones who were playing skins. Sneakers squeaking on the hot scuffed tar. The chain web of net rattling with each shot. The sun shined wetly off the skins' sweaty backs as they shouted and breathed hard, crowding with shoulders and thrusting hips to make a space, and high as I was, I felt safe admitting silently to myself that I wanted to drink greedily of that sweat, rivering in beads along the valleys of their spines while the boys shouted, while they shot and breathed hard.

In some ways I suppose I wasn't too different from a kid at the movies gobbling popcorn in a daze. Watching their scrimmage so intently, I was smoking my joint way too fast, getting way too high. But that's what the joint was for. It was the only means I had back then to make myself okay with what I was doing. It allowed me to want what I want. It gave me permission. And maybe if things had been different back then, it'd've been easier to cope with that want. I mean, everyone in school knew there was something going on with those basketball boys. The girls' team hated them, but everyone else seemed scared. After all, they were our jocks, and in the food chain extant in any American high school, jocks always are granted a specific height of respect. That's the rule. But these boys were fey and languid and the one guard kept his hair real long so that it bounced and streamed in a mane when he ran. They were the only boys in school who didn't shy away from physical contact. They were comfortable with the ubiquity of touch. And even in Phys Ed where the activity was barely measurable, barely active, they were always the first ones stripped and in the showers, always the last ones out. Never shying from the ubiquity of touch. And yet, they were champions. They made all of us champions. Which is why everyone was so scared of these boys. They were horses. But they were pink horses. And more than anything, I longed hard to be one of them.

But of course, I couldn't play ball. I couldn't go out for sports at all. Doctor's orders. I was and still am a hemophiliac. My body too willing and eager to bleed out. And even now, having had all my life to get used to the fact, I still sometimes get confused and say hypochondriac instead. Which is different. But sometimes I wonder: How different? Maybe I'm not actually confused. Maybe my body is the hypochondriac. Always convinced it's dying when really, all it is is feeling.

The shiny boy with the long hair stole the ball from a blonde ox in a FUBU T and ran backwards real quick, almost to the center line. Then he sank a three-pointer. He didn't even jump. He shot with his left hand. The babies squealed and rolled down the hill with no one to care whether or not they were safe, the shiny wet boy landed his impossible three-pointer, and I—deliciously high and permitting, permitting on my seventeenth birthday—I kneaded my crotch and shot off down my pant leg.

It's always so amazing, how swift and transformative release can be. And you know, I used to confuse "touched" with "blessed" back then, too, when to say one and when to say the other. "That boy is touched." "That boy is blessed." Forgetting which one meant he was special and which one meant he was defective. But I don't make that mistake anymore.

Across the field, on the court, the shirtless boys all shouted, "Triple-Double! Triple-Double!" and closed in around the boy with the gilt mane of hair. They engulfed him in their naked arms. All their torsos touched.

But that was just the cherry. I didn't need any more. I'd released, and I'd transformed. Muscles loose and lungs able to breathe. Until my high was gone, I would not feel any shame. I got up from the grass feeling like an orange oak leaf caught up in desiccating wind. I headed back home along the abandoned rails. Leaving the boys to celebrate themselves. Leaving the babies to roll and roll again.

Sometimes when I think back on it, I let the filmstrip in my mind end there, the sweaty boys having served their purpose. But Mom was awake when I crossed the grass back home. Sitting up half-in and half-out of the open back door. Hooded eyes kind of swollen like she was maybe still half-asleep. Smiling to herself with golden hair unraveling in spirals to frame her cheeks.

All around the yard, the house's shadow lay cooling and dim. I came around the Eagle's wide-open door and kissed my mom in the part of her hair, and she hummed and wished me happy birthday. If she smelled the dope smoke clinging to my everything, she never let on. She took my hand and I helped her stand and we walked like that through the dragonflies and shade over to my cake in the grass, knelt on either side of the broken chair and stared at that chocolate wheel. Waiting for the clock to run out. Waiting for the last bell. Very likely, Mom felt as dopey as I did right then. Summer and sleep and dust. Most of the time, my insides feel like they've been caught and wound tight in a flywheel. But for a moment, this wasn't the case. For the first time all day, I think I actually felt happy. I felt happy looking at my mom. Her sleepy eyes and all her curls. All her golden curls.

No doubt those boys on the courts were touched. But they were also blessed. All the world thought there was something wrong with them because of things they could not hide. But their being wrong is what set them free. They were blessed by being touched.

So what then was I? Was I blessed, or was I touched? Then and now, the answer's the same. I'm neither. I'm not blessed. I am not touched. Of course I'm not.

Of course I'm not.

Mom looked away from the cake up at me and told me it was time. But there were no forks with the cake. No plates and no knife. All of that was inside the house. And we were outside. Mom's blue eyes locked on my eyes and I wanted to smile—really, I did—but I couldn't make it happen. All I could do was make a space between my lips, and breathe. But I guess that was enough. Slowly we lowered our faces to the wheel. It wasn't even worth pretending. We opened our mouths—summer sweetly already on our lips—and our open mouths took it all in.

SAW-WHET

Woke up this morning forgetting my own body to the shout of a crow outside the open window above the headboard of your bed, its shout followed far away across the lake by another crow shouting back. They'd found one another from across a reflecting distance, but were making no effort to cross the span. Just shouting the same thing at each other. Over and over again. But how can I know it's the same? I cannot hear the changes. I lay and listened to this argument of crows and thought about the water that kisses the stone, about the lake's breath misting up through the morning air—the things of which I was certain—and when I finally opened my eyes, I saw the near crow perched above me on the open window's sill, its black eyes fixed down at me spread naked across your copper sheets. It measured me with one feldspar eye, then the other. Then it shouted down at my face, and it sounded just the same as before. It'd been there all along, pealing its call above me into your cliff-side house. But faintly across the lake, I could still hear the other crow scream back.

It was noon by the time we reached your cabin but with all the black tree-shadows stretching all around, it could just as easily have been morning or early evening. I kept calling the trees pines and Honey kept correcting me, but I couldn't remember what the trees were really called so instead I just called them pines. She growled and hit me with a pinecone. To all of this, you just laughed, stippled light catching in your white hair, in your blue eyes like the wet moons spinning bright around Saturn. You said we were good company for an old man, that we kept you feeling young, and Honey seemed to like that but I didn't know how to feel. In the cabin, we opened all the doors and cranked up the shutters like eyelids covering the windows and shook out the blankets from the couches and the beds to make sure there were no spiders hidden in the folds. It felt like the cabin was made out of windows, like we might as well be outside. But you said that was wrong. It was the purpose of the illusion to hide our insideness. We felt we were free. But we were contained. Through the trees we could see the wooded cliff drop steeply down several hundred feet to the lake spreading out in all directions below us, a great misted mirror running up into the far-off shore where the cliffs and trees resumed and beyond that, like Viking thugs, the severe old mountains began. It was a prehistoric place, carved away by glaciers, and it felt like it, too. We didn't belong here. Nobody belonged here. We brought in our bags and our boxes of food and you and I were standing at a window watching some red-headed bird whacking its face into a tree when Honey began shouting excitedly outside, then rushed in saying she'd found bees. At first you thought maybe she meant hornets or wasps because most people don't know the difference. But you should have known. Up in a tree on a low branch not far from the house, Honey'd found a wild hive, bees piled in an oblong mass and climbing all over one another, but Honey knew: there was a comb inside. She found some resinous weed and twisted its sticky leaves together into a long cone, then lit the torch and approached the hive. Acrid smoke feathered up in a plume. I went back inside. I didn't want to see what happened next. I thought for sure she'd get stung to death, and headstrong as she was, there was nothing I could do to stop it, so I went inside and made the cans on the countertop into pointless rearrangements, but a few minutes later she strutted into the kitchen with you close behind, beaming like a proud child with a piece of comb upheld in her hand, veins of honey dripping the golden length of her wrist and of her arm. A long drip extended from her elbow. Then it dropped.

There is something in the movement of forest light angling through slow rivers of honey that is like the light that illuminates an icicle, dripping blue melt from an ice-dammed eave. Or anyway, is the opposite of that. Winter light's inverse glowing slowly through honey. But both are trapped and trapping. Throughout the winter, you would take us out to dinner two or three nights a week. Raw bars with glowing aquariums beneath the zinc counters and behind all the booths, Italian places with wine-stained linen draped over close round tables, cavern-ous steakhouses with endless antlers mounted on the pickleboard walls. Or just as often, we would cook for you at our place, air cloudy with pasta steam mixing its warm wet smell with the scent of Honey's houseplants, the pungency of geraniums and the rich darkness of potting soil. You'd sit on our couch beneath a bower of hoya vines and sip your wine and listen to our records, running your thumb along the paged edges of our books stacked to near tumbling, but you never looked inside. Then we'd eat. Pork belly ragout or glazed salmon steaks or, just once, a meatloaf like my stepmom makes with a ketchup sauce baked on top and oatmeal instead of breadcrumbs kneaded into the meat. You and Honey always had more to talk about. Her apothecary studies in tinctures and tonics overlapping with your past life as a book antiquarian, shelves dusty with the lore of folk long forgotten. You collaborated on telling stories, you familiar with the mythology surrounding this or that while Honey filled in the physical result: belief that verbascum clears the lungs, that a mouthful of spider webs will stop an asthma attack, that the hand of glory brined from a hanged man's hand could paralyze its possessor's enemies. I've never had a head for these things, what was true and what was superstition, but I loved hearing you two talk about it, filling the air with a library of knowledge most people do not know or even know to wonder about. I would listen and build an archive with my mind, collating all the indices without needing to know what it all meant, only caring what went together, what was unrelated and apart. Honey would squeeze an eyedropper of pressed rosemary or lilac or dandelion into your wine, telling you why you needed that particular potency right then, and you would act surprised and congratulate her prescience, knowing your hands hurt by the way you handled your fork, a burgeoning cold by only the color around your eyes. But there came a point when all that changed, and Honey's ministrations to you became private. You were there so you know these things but it is important that I repeat them so that they don't get lost. I am building a map of who we were. I am relearning the streets of my memory, the shortcuts between here and there. Honey and I were two young kids barely scraping by and you entered our life through our January door and accepted what you found living one floor below you, validated what we were hoping for, what we'd strove so far to become. When the weather warmed we would cook on our roof with a little hibachi grill, pieces of fish and vegetables and meat, and you told us how when you were a boy you nursed back to health a young saw-whet owl with a crippled foot and I remember that name because it was such a rare, strange sound in my ear and in my mouth. Saw-whet. Saw-whet. Saw-whet. You explained how tiny a bird it was, how it fit in the palm of your childhood hand. A miniature version of some fierce and powerful thing, riding a young boy's fist. For nights afterward, I dreamed of tiny owls nestled and silent inside all things. They were hidden.

After Honey gathered her comb from the hive, we all took naps in our rooms. Honey and I curled against one another in the eastern bedroom with filtered tree light falling all around us through the windows, her belly inflating with breath against my back while you lay in your southern room, door shut, maybe not asleep but just resting or reading a book. But nestled beside Honey, I imagined that you were just lying there, watching the ceiling and feeling the breeze move over you from the window, lost in thought or listening. The image scared me like something from a bad dream. I don't know why. Then I slept and dreamed I was back in the city, riding my bicycle along my routes, my basket full of packages but never stopping to drop them off. Only riding from place to place by the fluid memory of place, the map drawn only in my mind. Later, we made a dinner of many different fishes: we'd bought a slim filet of every fish they had outspread on the ice at the public market. We stood in a line at the long kitchen counter and prepared each one differently, a different glaze or sauce or rub for each pink or white or yellow slice, then grilled them outside over hot coals. We laid the pieces out on a single broad platter so the filets were like the spokes of some colorful wheel. Then we tore off pieces with a leaf of bibb lettuce or a hunk of warm bread or with daylily blooms Honey had harvested from a clutch behind the house, washing it all down with green wine. The whole afternoon felt like play. It didn't matter that we were adults. We nudged each other with our elbows and teased. We threw bread and flowers at each other across the table. Later, we fixed big bowls of fresh strawberries and whipped cream, and when we asked Honey about the honeybees' comb and why we were not having that with dessert, too, Honey smiled secretly and raised her glass and did not answer the question that both of us had asked.

The sound of a paddle thumping the bottom of a canoe can travel the whole length of a lake when it's calm. In the deserts of the Old World, eating a jackal's heart will curse your child into a coward. The crow has over forty distinct calls but by and large, we only ever hear one. If you cut one's tongue, it can learn to speak our words. The sight of small birds ascending the bark of a tree as easily as if it were a horizontal plane pleases you in a way that few other things can. The inquisitive hop of finches defying gravity, bound instead by curiosity to things much smaller than the world. You once owned an orange cat named Charlemagne who lost his eye under mysterious circumstances. He was the meanest creature you'd ever known. You could never stand the sound of a bike chain. These are the things you spoke of on our long ride up into the forests above the city. The way sunfish will nip your toes if you dangle your feet in the water off a dock. The sound of squirrels galloping across a roof. The refined joy of waking in a sunny room to the scent of coffee and pancakes being made elsewhere in the house. You took one hand away from the steering wheel and rotated your wedding band with the tip of your thumb. It didn't look like you knew you were doing it. It's an act, you said, that's more than just feeding, letting someone you love sleep in while you cook a good breakfast for them. It's more than just food.

Not once have you ever mentioned word one about your wife. But that January there was the storm that no one expected that dumped six feet of snow in a single afternoon and night. People got trapped in their offices or in their cars on the freeway and I got trapped at my stepmom's house in the suburbs south of the city because she'd asked me to come help move some boxes for her and then when I was there, the snow started to fly and in the morning I had to dig my bike free. Already by eight that morning, it had warmed into the forties, snow melting and compressing in a wet, heavy, half-itself. The main roads had been cleared but for cars, not for bikes. It was a slushy, harrowing ride. When I got to the park, I tried to cut through it, thought that would be safer, but all I managed was to get my bike stuck in a snow bank. I was really starting to panic because I had not seen or spoken to Honey since before the storm. I didn't know if she'd be okay. Four guys converged on me then, two from either direction, trudging through the snow where the sidewalk used to be, and at first I thought they'd hurt me but instead they helped me with my bike. One of the guys looked like he worked but the other three did not. All but two of them were strangers. They were older. After they helped pull my bike out of the snow, we stood talking about the storm. Specifically, about people's dogs. Not knowing the storm was coming until too late, or anyway not knowing it would be so bad, a lot of folks had left their dogs tied up in their yards. Some could barely stay up above the piling snow, their leads were so short. Some died. One man said he'd been lucky because his dog had a doghouse to take shelter in: when he got home, he had to dig it out of five feet of snow. It was happy to see him. I was getting more anxious to leave but felt captive since they'd helped me. The one guy who worked looked the same way. Finally, the two men who knew each other pointed out a path that cut diagonally through the park, foot-packed by others before us. I thanked them and pushed my bike through the park and rode the back streets up the hill, zigzagging toward home. I imagined Honey snowed-in and panicking. I imagined the power out, phones down, no water. The ceiling caving in. Strange men at the door. Honey slipping on ice and hitting her head and getting buried in yards of snow. Snow blind in the street then hit by a plow. By the time I reached our street, I believed all of it. I lugged my bike up the salty front steps of our building and wrestled it through the doors, locked it in the entry and ran all the way up to the fourth floor, but when I poured into the apartment panting and almost in tears, the lights were on and the apartment was warm and Honey was serving you tea at our table. Everything was fine. Honey seemed surprised to see me. But you just smiled. I could see all the creases around your eyes.

So I guess that's when we first met. After dinner and strawberries we followed the winding trail down the cliff from the cabin to the water and got a canoe out of the boathouse and put it in the lake, then fitted a small trolling motor to the canoe. You said you were too old for paddling, but I said you're not that old. Honey stayed behind and we pushed off into the clear still water, and the engine purred in a way that made you forget it was even there, and I thanked you for coming over that time in the storm to make sure Honey was okay, even though you'd never met, were just neighbors on different floors. You said it was nothing, it's what people do in a storm, check in on each other, or anyway it's what people used to do, but then you wondered out loud if anyone ever really did that, looked out for one another, or if it's just something we do, this contagious romanticizing of the past. I said I didn't know, but I hope my memories are true. There were not many cabins on the lake. I watched trees and rocks go by, the occasional dock. I heard loons and a few seconds later saw them drifting on the water. They'd float placid and still then all at once dive. They would surface again later somewhere else. Something like a dinosaur winged by high overhead and I pointed and you said it was a heron. I was very unused to these things. I liked that you had answers. I told you about a time when I was still a girl and my brother and I went someplace we shouldn't have. We'd lied and told our stepmom we were going to a particular library on the hill, but when we got to the hilltop, we rode down its steep south face into a neighborhood that was mostly abandoned. We locked our bikes to a chain-link fence and started trying doors. There was an apartment building whose side door was open but all the apartments were locked. I remember the sound of our feet pounding up and down the concrete stairwell, and the red paint on the metal railing. We went into a few houses and for a while a girl my brother knew joined us but then she left. That was the only other person we saw down there. All the houses were clean and empty but obviously had once been lived in. We couldn't understand where all the people had gone. Then it started raining and we stood in the living room of one house waiting for it to pass. The room was painted a pale orange or dark yellow and that color even now still reminds me of the Cold War. Like the metal railing and concrete steps. A certain careless lack of adornment, like we were expecting the bomb to erase everything soon anyway. I stood beside my brother by the window in an abandoned house, and we watched the rain falling outside. We could see the harbor from here. Boats moving in the rain. We didn't say anything. We waited.

You asked me what made me think of that now. I said you remind me of my brother sometimes. You both know things that I don't. There was an island ahead of us in the lake and first we moved toward it and then when we got there, we started to go around. You said there's all sorts of stuff that I don't know and stuff you don't know either. We both might have answers to the other's questions. But if neither asks, neither has to tell. All the ride up from the city to your cabin, wind ripping in through the windows and blowing through everyone's hair, it'd been like one long joke, all of us laughing, no matter what was said, always laughing. But it sometimes seemed like only you and Honey were privy to the joke. Which was fine: you two were friends first before I met you, if only by a few hours. I guessed it was this, our questions and answers, you were talking about.

On the far side of the island, as we rounded its jutting point—so thinly forested you could see sky between the scraggly branches of the trees—we saw a moose swimming from the mainland to the island, its rack above the water like some monstrous crab floating on the lake. You saw what it really was before I did. You cut the motor and we drifted while it swam by. It didn't look at us as it passed. It must be hard swimming with hooves instead of hands. When it reached the narrow finger of the island, it trotted up the rocks taller than I imagined it could be and shook off and clopped in among the trees, all knobby knees and skinny legs. I wondered out loud why it would do that. You said you didn't know. We rounded the island and headed back toward the cabin after that. The sun had gotten much lower while we coursed through the still water and now was nearly gone behind a mountain. That part of the sky was all orange and red like a blister of molten stone. Everything else was variations on black. The liquid black of the lake. The opaque black of land. Vaporous black in the sky to the east but softly luminous purple everywhere else. There were almost no lights lining the edge of the lake and none on the water and a flash of panic lanced through me as I wondered if we'd find our landing in the dark, and without thinking I muttered my stepmom's favorite lines from Job, about God's favoritism falling on the Leviathan and the Behemoth among all His creatures. Humans didn't even come close. But you didn't hear me or must have misunderstood, because it was almost like you were barking in the near silence of the lake, the sharp way you asked, "What did you just say to me?" But I wouldn't say it again.

We found the landing and hauled the boat in then started the long walk up the cliff to the cabin. It was darker there among the trees, but as we'd been in the dark so long, we'd adjusted and could see the gravel path almost glowing, leading us up, the bushes and trees pouring on either side. You were breathing hard but laughing about it. Whatever nastiness that had just passed in the boat was forgotten. I teased you and said I thought Honey and I were keeping you young. And you laughed and said not that young. All the windows were glowing with a warm and yellow light and when we came in Honey hugged and kissed us both on the lips and said we were just in time, she'd prepared something warm for us to drink. Agastache blooms from her window box at home, and elderflower and raspberry leaf she'd found in the woods around the cabin, and hot water and bourbon. A gooey piece of honeycomb floated in each of our mugs. You laughed when she told you what was in the tea. You said raspberry was for easing birthing pains. But Honey just grinned, said nothing. Touched her fingers to your mug and pushed it toward your mouth. You drank and we all drank and you laughed and said you were glad to have met us when you did in your life. It was only just a few months ago that the storm came and brought us together. But these few months felt like a lifetime. A whole new and brief and complete life. You said you were grateful for that. You said you were glad we were all here together on the lake. Then you finished your drink in a single long draft but did not chew up the comb. You took the mug with you into the north room that was really all glass looking out over the whole lake and forest and the mountains after that. You went to the couch set against the north wall of glass and sat and then lay down. You held the mug between your hands on the table of your chest. I guess you could smell the melting honey inside. There was still a faint little light on the lake, a red outline of the fallen sun outlining the farthest mountains, but the way you lay on the couch, you couldn't see any of that. Your head was pointed west and your feet were pointed east. Like you were more interested in seeing the sun rise tomorrow than in watching it fade today. You closed your eyes and for a moment you rested, and a little while later, you were dead.

Honey came in and knelt beside you on the floor. She took the mug of honeycomb from your hands and set it by her knees, then held your hands and cried some but not much. I stood a little way off and watched. It was dark out now and I could see nothing of the lake, could only see my reflection in the black windows, the whole cabin repeated in dim reverse. I found a blanket and laid it over you but did not cover your face. It was an Indian blanket, alternating valleys and peaks of deep red and orange and electric blue and brown. Tucked in like that, with your hands still on your chest, you looked asleep. But for a moment, I thought you'd burst open with owls. One thousand tiny saw-whets, hidden behind your chest. I touched Honey's shoulder and she stood and we hugged, then went into the other room.

There was no phone in the cabin. I could remember the route we took up from the city, but it'd be hard to retrace our path in the dark. We didn't know what towns had police stations or hospitals or even where we were supposed to go. We decided we'd wait until morning to take you down the cliff. There wasn't any hurry anymore. We sat in the kitchen and had another drink. Honey asked about the canoe, but I didn't know the answer. Then she began wondering out loud about the lake. How many thousands or millions of years old it was. How it had been shaped. If there was life here in the world at the time or if that came later. How life eventually found it, fish in the water and birds in the trees. How can any life find anything that's so far away? How did we? Honey cried some then and I held her and then we kissed for a while but decided that night we each wanted to sleep alone. We turned out the lights and it was dark so we turned a couple back on, and Honey slept in the room we'd picked out earlier and I slept in your room. I remember, the bed was unmade, blanket and sheet pulled back. Like a letter that'd been read then returned to its envelope, open. I took off my clothes and lay in your sheets and dreamed of water gushing out of a stone, raging and white and filling up a space roughly scraped from between two mountains. There were no people and there were no trees. Just clear water rushing to flood a valley. Climbing the mountain walls. Then I awoke naked in the morning's still light and did not remember what had happened and then in a moment I did and I saw the crow above me in the open window, shouting into this space you'd brought us to while somewhere faraway and unseen, another crow shouted back, hoping it would be heard.

SKIDDER & DRAW

My stepfather and I went down the hill to the wood lot behind the house, thinking to make firewood from some trees. I manned the skidder while he worked the saw—diesel smoke and two-stroke smoke and the green scent of sawdust hanging bright in the October air—and within the first few minutes, he and I each nearly died at the other's hand. I had hopped down from the machine, tugging a cable from the braid to noose around a felled tree, when a down-sweeping birch whooshed alongside me to the ground. Its topmost leaves brushed down my face, the length of my chest, my legs. My stepfather hadn't seen me leave the machine. If it'd fallen a moment sooner—if I'd been a couple feet closer—I'd've fallen with it. But it didn't, and I hadn't, so I was fine. We regarded each other wide-eyed from opposing ends of the clearing. Then I noosed the tree I'd come for and ran a cable to the new birch too, jogged back to the skidder and winched them both in, and it was while I struggled to lock the machine into gear, aiming to drag the pull to the timber pile around the bend, that my stepfather stepped up alongside me. But I didn't see him there. I jumped the clutch and the skidder stalled, its big back wheel lunging forward just enough to nudge my stepfather's shoulder hard, then roll back. It could so easily have kept mowing forward. He staggered a step and stared at the wheel, his expression all askance, like a stranger had come up and poked him unprovoked. Then he looked up at me. It was a long still moment where neither of us said a word. We both knew. In his one hand, the chainsaw burbled and coughed. I turned the engine over, and it fired. We both went back to work.

BLUE OF THE WORLD

May 24th, 1965

Walked the orchard line with the boy today after the service, from the house to the north end of the property. All the blooms had blown off the limbs so just a foamy wash of white or dried-up yellow petals were left here and there on the ground. Very many small green apples have started, few much bigger than the head of a nail. The trees looked good. I do not much fear a late frost ruining everything that's begun. But in this, I've been wrong before.

The land very slightly inclines to the north here so it was harder going up than coming back. We collected blowdowns as we followed the single straight file of trees, stacking them on a sledge the boy pulled. I brought a saw in case we needed to clear a split limb from a live tree. We needed the saw twice. Mules grazed nearby with the jack donkey in the pasture east of us and after a spell, were joined by the quarter horses. We'd been discovered. Just post and board fence between us and them, they following as we worked the orchard line. We must have been good fun to watch. I suggested we hitch the sledge to any one of them—it's easy work for a horse and not work at all for a mule—but the boy said no.

The pasture west of the orchard has grown meadow-sweet and fallow with tall grass. If I can mend the fences on that side of the trees, I will swap the beasts over there. But I'm not certain I have that ambition yet this year.

At the northern boundary line where our land meets the Finnegans', we rested and ate sandwiches and shared cold coffee from a jelly jar. We agreed, the coffee was not as good as it used to be. Something missing, or the ratios wrong. It's hard to enjoy a thing when your memory of it is sweeter. Toward the faraway hills, men were standing the first girders of a new weather tower. The sight of it makes me hate. We finished our lunch and coffee and headed back south to the house, looking for anything we missed along the way. The horses followed.

May 25th, 1965

Taught the boy how to mend the leather of a stirrup torn free from its fender. He is still too short to work at the bench with ease.

May 28th, 1965

John Henneker has called every day for the past two weeks, begging me to bring a sire out to rut his dam Dilly, and only just yesterday offered to pay me for this service. Being neighbors entitles us to nothing of each other. He must have just got the news. He named what he could pay and I told him what that could buy him. He didn't seem too picky. Chose a young painted stud, barely more than a colt. Never been sired. Quick and leggy. Rambunctious and maybe a little dumb. It all sounded fine to John. All he asked is that it be pretty.

The Henneker farm is a twenty mile drive or more but only fifteen if one draws a straight line between our two places, and anyway they weren't expecting us at any particular time, so the boy and I saddled up our Ghost and Coyote before dawn and led the paint by a rope from the team. Among the wild parti-colors of quarter horses, there's a wordless rare something in riding tall milk-white Saddlebreds. It's best in the dark before sunrise, when you're the only white thing in the world glowing like a moon. It's good to feel you're a rare riding thing some-times, even if you aren't. We took turns holding the paint's rope: when we crossed a property, we'd switch. Headed north along the orchard line and crossed onto the Finnegans' land, down their pasture and through the wooded way and along the west shore of their wide, muddy cattle pond, then up the grassy slope and across a dirt road onto the Halls' land where things flatten and dry out nicely. It's a piece of land that'd be more at home two hundred miles west of here, in Interior or Kadoka. No good for pasture or growing much more than pigweed and morning glory and really, given the rockiness, not the safest riding. A horse can twist an ankle on a loose stone as easily as a man can. But it feels correct. The sun was still low so the earth looked more purple and blue than anything else. Now and then, a spooked rabbit would dart off ahead of us and disappear. It was ghostly, that flash of rabbit. Far away, we could see the big hills rolling. The boy had once said they looked like someone lying with a blanket pulled up over her face. But he didn't say anything today. Told him, back east, people called these mountains. He said he knew, I'd told him that before.

We took the horses easy on that sweet flat piece, then watered them at Cane Brook. That marked the boundary between the Halls' and Hennekers' lands. But we still had a ways to go. We traded the paint's rope and crossed the brook, up a rock bank under a canopy of cottonwoods, then into a pasture that'd grown wild with disuse. The Hennekers, I believe, have more land than their cattle can manage for them. John needs to up his herd. Or let some bison in. Then again, I should not be so quick to advise unasked, as much of my land to the west looks just the same as this. That pasture—though I guess it's really straight reclaimed prairie—ran all the way to the farm-house. There were eventually beef cattle grazing who'd look at us curiously as we passed. Great black and crimson cows. The grass was shorter near the farm.

The younger two Henneker boys met us at the gate and took Ghost and Coyote into the barn, their little sister chasing along after. I believe she was intent on brushing them. It was beginning to make sense to me why John wanted his dam foaled so bad. A girl child had lit a fire under his ass for something pretty to ride. He didn't give a damn what kind of horse he fostered as long as it was a horse. I felt fine with my choice of sire. John Henneker came along a moment later, worrying his fingers with a dirty red rag, then shook my hand and the boy's hand and admired the paint entirely on its color and shape. He did not look at its teeth, and I was glad. It's always a favor when folk don't pretend to know something. I explained to him the horse was not really a Paint, just painted. He looked at me like I was a moron. John's wife Evelyn came out after that and asked if we'd like something to eat or drink. We did. We had coffee and cold lunch in their kitchen and when we were done, we took the sire to a paddock where Henneker's bay draft horse Dilly was waiting. We let the two of them figure it out from there.

We stood there leaning against the wood fence, watching. Me and the boy and John Henneker and Evelyn. I was prepared to leave the paint for a day or more to give them time to adjust to one another, but they proved to make pretty fast friends. The two horses circled and sniffed each other, then the dam lifted her tail and pissed and the sire sniffed the piss, then sniffed its source and climbed on. He was a solid three hands shorter than she and just about fell off on his first attempt. But it's a lesson each of us eventually learns. It wasn't long before they got it all worked out.

John paid me after that. You could tell he'd made a special trip to the bank just for this. Crisp new bills still bound in a paper band. While we shook hands, John's youngest two—one boy and one girl—led out our rides by their bridles. Both horses looked well brushed. The girl was leading the boy's horse. She knew it. It pleased the boy and she knew that, too. We mounted then led the sire by his rope out the gate, and he seemed a little more frolicky than usual. The rutting has put some pep in him. Trotted out of the used pasture then galloped when we hit the disused part. Everyone seemed happy for the speed.

Heading back, we took a different route home. The sun was angling lower, making everything bright green and golden. The horses shook their heads and made sounds, as if they found it pleasing to try an untrod path. Once on our own land, we cut southwest past the orchards into a pasture grown tall and wild. We rode until we reached our cold water pond, big flat rocks and silt at its edges. Narrow creek nuzzling out of the shallows, acting casual sneaking southwest to join up with its friends and rush wicked into the Missouri. In its middle, you could see the pond's face purling where the spring boiled up underneath. I can remember a time when the boy would ask where the water came from, how come it was always there. I know as much about it now as I did then. We tied the horses to a bone-dry and uprooted cottonwood root, then took off our clothes and swam. The boy was laughing. He could slice through the water like some silvery, brown-eyed fish. He did not learn this from me. I am all mammal in water, built to push through it, get to the other side. Have to remind myself that this is not a job. But the boy needs no reminding. Dive to the bottom and come up with rocks, little white twists that might be ancient bone. He's teaching me what is fun. I'd crouch in shallow water up to my chin and he'd balance his feet in the stirrup on my hands. Then I'd stand up quick, and launch him.

June 1ˢᵗ, 1965

Every morning, there's a great revival of birds singing all at once in the orchard trees and pastures. See them lined up on the crossbeams of our tin-can scarecrow in the garden. Watch them slice shapes in the air. They never stop singing when they fly. They will light on the backs of sleeping horses and sing. I do not know if they understand what the other birds are saying, or if they even understand themselves.

I have never known the name of any bird other than a crow. But the boy knows. He is learning. There's a library book with colored pictures, and a record of the songs they sing. It's one of the things he studies. He'll put on the record and page through the book. Our house filled with the songs of singing birds. He knows the names that people use and the Latin names used only by doctors and poets. He feels it is his inheritance and responsibility, the naming of all the birds when there's no one else here who can name them anymore.

June 2nd, 1965

Drove the boy to the library. He's a collector now of everything. Engine design and Iron Age wars and big books of maps, places I never heard of. Asked him on the ride home if he minded that I'd taken him out of school for so long. He said no, he didn't mind, but by fall he'll want to go back. He knows what this is about. I hope I'll be ready by then.

June 4th, 1965

Today came the man from the big Montana ranch with his two trucks hauling long gooseneck trailers. We had spoken on the phone. This was expected. Sort of waddled when he hopped down out of his truck, but the other driver didn't even turn off his engine. Without these deals now and then to big ranches, an operation small as ours would go under in a season. It saves us. Even still, it saddens me to see so many animals gone in one day. I feel a closeness to these things. Quarter horses and mules. Strange animals like great dogs with hooves, both sweet and wild. The Montanan had the specs of his order and it'd have been easy enough for the boy and I to gather in his horses—they are familiar with us and don't worry when we cull any one of them from the team—but the Montanan wanted to have a physical role in their selection. Which made it a true culling. They ran. We spent the morning chasing them in circles, cutting horses out one at a time. It was a waste of time, and it scared the beasts. But the Montanan felt very proud of his efforts and his active hand in the choosing. The work was a joy for him because it was his choice to work. The boy kept arrowing glances my way, like he wanted me to say something, stand up to this pot-bellied rich man. I couldn't rightly tell him then that this one sale would spell easy sailing for the rest of the year. So I held my tongue and cut the horses one by one and later forgot to explain. So I guess he still sees me more as a coward than a businessman.

For letting him pretend he was a cowboy, the rancher threw in a bonus. Then he took his sixteen head of skittish horses and went back to Montana. The boy said he wished that lost sixteen luck. I take that to be his way of saying that he was not fond of the fat man. It was long after dark when what was left of my team finally lost fear and grew still.

June 5*th*, 1965

I let the boy sleep more lately than I did when he went to school. There really isn't enough work now for two men. I can do the rote chores in the morning while he sleeps. Save the more interesting work to tackle later on as a team. But even with these dawn chores, I'm learning to take my time. This morning I went out onto the porch with my coffee, thinking I'd watch the blue world take on all its colors with the sun, but as soon as I stepped out, I saw on the deck boards a little grey lump. A big black beetle was rolling the lump around. Sometimes burying its head into a softness. And as it moved the lump around, I realized what I was seeing was a very small, very dead bird. I do not know what bird it was. It hadn't any feathers to speak of, just the moldy fuzz of a hatchling. The beetle unfolded the bird's bunched-up neck and articulated its clenched legs. I know the beetle was just feeding, but it seemed it was trying to reanimate the bird. As if by exercising its limbs, it could bring it back to life. I crouched there on the porch watching the beetle work to resuscitate this little rotten thing. Then I went back inside. Without my noticing, the blue of the world was gone.

But a curiosity was in me now. Took the little ash shovel down from its place by the wood stove and went back outside, scooped the bird and beetle up. Set them on a stump behind the house where I once had to cut an old rock elm down. Figured they'd be safe over there. Keep an eye on them now and then without worrying the boy might find them. I don't know how he'd react to this sort of thing. I'm not sure how I'm reacting myself.

June 6th, 1965

Thought I saw you hanging laundry today. Wind whipping the white sheets to snapping at your heels. But it was just the boy. Doing the job you used to do.

June 8th, 1965

The boy went out to pick alpine strawberries (or as my ma used to call them, *fraises des bois*) with the Hautenot girl this morning in the Kelloggs' fields south of here, so I took the truck into town. I needed nails and coffee and thought maybe I'd see what else they got at the store that we've never tried before. I think it's good for the boy to try new things. I do not like being in that house all alone. Went to the hardware store and got some nails and a new leather punch as mine has mysteriously grown bent (a mystery I'm sure the boy knows the solution to) then talked to Henry for a spell and had an RC Cola because business was slow for Henry and I was in no hurry. He didn't have anything worth saying to say. At the Hy-Vee, got the coffee and a box of pancake mix because I can't make them right from scratch—there is something I'm missing that I cannot get right—and nothing else looked interesting so I bought a giant Southern watermelon. It was shaped like a box. I suspected the boy would get a kick out of that. The girl working checkout was pretty and smiled at me a lot. But I couldn't really smile back. I'm not ready yet for that kind of attention, it does no good for me now. So I didn't look at her at all. I hope she understands.

Driving home, waiting at a red light, I happened to notice a little orange butterfly flying circles round above the pavement. It was new tar macadam there. It was black. The butterfly kept circling the same patch of road like there was something there it liked. But there was nothing there. Then a worrying thing happened, as I started feeling a sort of panic tightening up in my throat. Just off the shoulder, there were flowers growing in the grass, and not far past that, fields of flowers. So why was this butterfly circling hot tar? Maybe there wasn't anything there where it was circling, but there used to be. Maybe it was remembering something that was long gone, paved over and buried. What I understand is that butterflies are always heading somewhere, either to or from some breeding ground in Mexico. But this one wasn't going anywhere. Just circling where something used to be. I was scared it might die by this choice. Get burned up on the sun-hot tar or hit any second now by a car. The world is too much for an animal so small to make choices that aren't only survival. The light had turned green but I hadn't noticed. Then someone behind me leaned on their horn. I wanted to save that stupid damn bug. But I couldn't. I couldn't even try. I drove through the light and brought the melon home to our boy.

June 10th, 1965

The dead bird moves a lot in the night. If it lay along the northeast rings of the stump at dusk, it'll be in the southern rings by morning. It's as if the beetle is passing coded messages, divining the weather, spelling good omens I hope. And too: there is a dead spider on the stump now as well. I don't know what killed either of these things. Only know they are gathering here.

June 13th, 1965

Ronald Haskell called about renting one of the mules to pull a load of wood he aims to fell in the back quarter of his property. Told him for an extra two hundred dollars, he could have a mule and keep it. It was a good deal for him, but I don't think he wanted it. I felt like a bully, sticking so firm to my offer. All mule or no mule. He came and got his animal before suppertime.

Later, the boy and I took Ghost and Coyote out in the west pastures. Sometimes trotting the horses and sometimes letting them run. It was aimless, the paths we took. Mostly let the beasts decide. The sky was liquid bright with colors but the dark lay low to the ground, almost black, everything just an outline of a shape. Shape of the boy. Shape of a tree. Far out, we saw some scavenger birds cutting circles in the air, so we rode out to see what we'd find. Dead doe splayed out in the grass, its hindquarters mostly ate off. A look of permanent terror fixed on its eyeless face. It stank. Ghost and Coyote stamped in the grass and threw their heads. They hated it.

Heading back, the boy pointed out the weather tower, getting taller. But I didn't want to see it. I spat.

June 14ᵗʰ, 1965

We were stripping an old saddle down to its tree when the boy asked me if we were ever going to talk about it. Didn't seem to me there was anything to talk about. But I didn't even say that. I showed him where the skirt tied into the tree. Then I cut the seam.

I believe he's beginning to resent me. He didn't like learning that Ron Haskell had taken the mule for keeps. He's been spending more time with the Hautenot girl.

That scrawny whippet with all the teeth. Over dinner, he stressed to me how much he was looking forward to starting school again in the fall. We both pretended like school wasn't still in session for everybody other than him.

After the boy went to bed, I stood out in the yard awhile listening to the wind and the horses and the rattle of the tin cans hanging in the scarecrow and what I assume was an owl calling, though it wasn't how I imagine an owl ought to sound. Then I went inside and found a lantern and headed off west past the orchards, tall grass hushing around my knees. I did not light the lamp until I got to our pond. I followed the horse paths there. Took off my clothes and folded them and set them in a pile beside the lantern on a flat rock. Then I went for a swim. The half-moon was high and set the water sparkling and I swam to the far side and back three times and on the fourth pass stopped and tread water in the center. There was nothing else out there. Just me and the water and the moon and the lamp. The lamp was only there so I could find the shore again when I was done. You couldn't see the far hills. Just prairie in all directions forever. But nothing felt far away. It was all right there with me. In the water or close to shore. The moon and lantern and the cold spring beneath my feet. Everything right there with me. I stayed as long as the cold water would let me. Then I swam to the light and got dressed and walked home, the lantern now dark in my hand.

Across the distance, I saw the kitchen light was on. You were sitting at the table when I walked in, playing solitaire and drinking a glass of ginger ale in your hospital gown. It's the last thing I'd seen you wearing. Two moths fluttered about the yellow light above your head. There were eyes of wet on your glass. I smiled and took my boots off and said hello, and you smiled at me and waved and said nothing. Your skin was very grey but your eyes were still cool like wet slate. Mouth tight and twisted like you were holding back a laugh. You gathered the cards and shuffled. I found a dusty bottle of Canadian Club in a high cupboard shelf and poured myself a glass and poured a splash in yours. I sat across from you at the table and you dealt out the cards. I wanted very badly to touch you. Your blonde hair was stringy and kept falling in your face. I wanted to tuck it behind your ear, touch the hollow where your jaw bends to meet your neck. But I didn't. I knew that was against the rules. There were dark bruises inside your elbows and on the back of your hands where the IVs had gone in. There was still a paper bracelet around your narrow wrist. A bird's wrist. We played a few hands of Rummy, matching runs and pairs. Then you asked me where I've been and I told you I went for a swim in the pond. But you shook your head and said that's not what you meant. I could see your knee peeking beneath the edge of your hospital gown and without thinking reached to touch it with the tip of my finger, the acre of my palm, but you shook your head again. Then you were gone.

I sat for a long time in the kitchen beneath the moths spinning in the light, my hair still wet from the pond. It was cold. Even with the night still and the wind far away, this house creaks like old bones. The unseen motions of ancient things. I turned out the light and went to bed.

June 18th, 1965

The boy told me today that I am stupid for selling the mule. We were weeding our small garden, culling the little shoots of jewelweed and pigweed and plantain from among the potato mounds and pea vine and bush beans. He said that I was getting it all backward. Said we ought to have lent the mule to the Haskells for free as a favor, and only charged him if the beast got hurt or took ill. He insisted that favors are worth more than dollars, as the price of gold goes up and down but a favor is always a favor. At the very least, we should have traded services, as the Haskells raise good hay and oats, and they needed the mule to haul wood, all of which are things we will need come wintertime. But regardless: we should not have sold the mule.

I said to him that I suppose he thinks we ought to have let our paint rut with the Henneker's dray for free, too. And I should fix every saddle and bridle and harness for whoever comes begging at our door. He agreed the leatherwork ought to cost, but to charge to let an untested colt plow a draft horse for no other purpose than to make an animal whose only job will be to be an animal? He thought it was a pointless and mean thing, asking money for that.

I reminded him that what we ran was a horse farm. Then he did something that surprised me. He was squatting down in the potato mounds, but he'd stopped picking weeds. He was looking at his hands in the cool, dark earth. Then he said that people's sympathy for me was wearing thin. He said I was eating up our neighbors' goodwill by being a greedy fly.

I told him sympathy was another name for cancer. I'd be happier when it was gone.

The boy stood up and chucked a clod of rotten seed potato at me. It sailed over my shoulder and struck the line of tin cans strung to our scarecrow crucifix. Then he marched out of the garden. Headed south. I suspect to go play with that homely Hautenot girl.

I finished weeding my row of peas. I worked in the barn on a new bridle and traces set. I stood in the orchard and listened to the nicker of horses, the scream of birds. I did not go into the house. I stood with the wind pushing my shoulders and tugging at my clothes. Then I got into the truck and drove. I didn't go anywhere. There was nowhere I wanted to go. I drove the dirt roads between farms and fields and looked out at the cattle standing still and chewing. I watched the sun melt off in the hills and the silver flint of moon rise up. Stars and the occasional mercury lamp burning cold over a closed barn door. I drove until very late before turning and heading back. I could smell the sweet dust gusting off the road as I passed along. Hoped the boy would be home when I got there.

June 20th, 1965

Afternoon clouds got dark all at once and a warm wind blew in hard and wet from the south. An uneasiness breathed in by the weather. I'd been sleeping but something woke me. Like a cool hand tracing down my neck. Looked to see what it was but saw nothing. Then I saw what was happening outside. Looked for the boy but could not find him so called but he wouldn't call back. The scarecrow's tin cans banged together like the drums in an Indian's dance. In the pastures, the horses were running hard, making noise, being beasts. The mules faced the wind and were mules. I saddled Circle as she hadn't been rode in some time and took to the fallow pastures at a steady beat and found the boy up in a box elder southwest of the farm. It was a squat arthritis tree with the pale undersides of its leaves turned up. It was the only tree around. Just a lot of tall grass lying flat beneath the wind. The boy's face was all wet and he wouldn't look at me.

This was nothing I'd thought him liable to still do, to runaway and to cry. I wasn't sure how to react to that. I did not like him in the tree. As he was on a low branch and I was on your horse, we were just about on a level with each other. I reached out and patted his shoulder. But I felt like a little league coach doing that, consoling a batter after striking out on an unimportant play. I suspected that sentiment was incorrect. He didn't look hurt, so I assumed it must be the other thing. The wind was getting worse and there was some deep animal sound coming from the clouds. It was a mean thing to say, but I told him to stop that now. Then I reached out and put an arm behind his back and pulled him onto Circle ahead of me on the saddle. He was too old for that kind of thing. But we had to move. I put the heels to your horse and we rode hard and fast back to the house. The quarter horses were acting like horses again, calm with the wind whipping back their mane. The jack donkey was chewing oats. They didn't care. They could handle themselves. We disrobed Circle and set her and Ghost and Coyote loose in the pasture with the others. Three white horses among varnished sorrels and blue roans and charcoal blacks underneath an evil marble of storm. Then we went inside, and first it hailed but then it rained in dark ribbons so you could see it wind like snakes through the air while far to the south, though we couldn't tell how far, we watched a black tornado touch down and ride.

June 21ˢᵗ, 1965

The bird is less lump and more skeleton now. No sign of the beetle. Where'd he go?

June 22ⁿᵈ, 1965

A full month or more after all the others had passed, the last late dam foaled today. I'm sure she had her reasons, but as they're horse reasons, I wasn't made privy. The boy'd been feeding sugar cubes to the quarter horses when he saw what was happening and ran back to the house. In his excitement, he forgot he wasn't talking to me. Put in the call to Dr. Vining, then saddled Ghost and Coyote and culled the dam real easy from the team. Put her in a paddock behind the stables. There was just a pale blue bubble like a misplaced balloon swelling out from her sex. But in the balloon there were hooves. She circled once slowly the paddock's dusty edge then lay herself down in the shade.

It wasn't much longer after that and with little more to do but to watch. Dr. Vining showed up and waved his hat and took up alongside us at the fence. Had only called him in in case there was trouble with the afterbirth. There weren't. The dam passed the foal and licked off its blue membrane then passed the afterbirth and ate that too. She nuzzled the foal until it found its feet and wobbled and had its first feeding. The dam was all chestnut with white showing on her ribs but the foal was buckskin, pale on its underside with a diamond between its eyes. After it fed, it gamboled a bit, ungainly but excited like it'd been looking forward to this chance to finally stretch out.

Dr. Vining refused any payment. Said he was happy to have been useless in the presence of such an easy birth. An uncommon twitchiness meanwhile was torturing the boy. He does not normally get worked up over new foals, but today on all accounts seems to be an exception. Said he'd like to ride out and fetch his friend, the Hautenot girl, as to show her the new foal. So maybe his excitement was on loan from her. Girls and horses. As she'd be riding back with him, I suggested he bring Circle along. They'd then each have their own ride. This seemed to please him, too. I hope he remembers this, that I am not always so contemptible. Saddled up Circle and mounted Coyote and took off with both horses across the southern fields. Watching them go, Dr. Vining laughed and said what a hell of a boy and I laughed with him and agreed, though I could only suspect what the doctor was commenting on. It didn't matter. Maybe I was starting to feel some of this contagious animal excitement as it was with a sudden burst of good feeling that I asked the doctor if he'd like to stick around for a spell, have a coffee or take a quick ride. Said he wished he could but duty called. He did not say what duty, though. He said my name and started his pickup and in a moment he was gone and very suddenly the farm felt emptied. I was still smiling in the yard but there was nothing to smile at. All at once, I was alone.

Went and checked on the foal and dam and found them sleeping in the dust, bellies rising big with deep, sleepy breaths. It's always made me uneasy, seeing horses sleeping but not standing, lying on the ground like they're dead. In the pasture, the mules and horses had gathered as close as they could to watch. Looked at their black eyes all pointed at me and could not know what they saw. Walked through the stables, sweet with the faint hay and manure smells, but vacant for the summer so feeling abandoned and forgot. The few slit-eyed barn cats here and there did not ease this deserted feeling. My brief flash of excitement was gone. People take it with them when they go. Stood out in the dooryard looking west, wondered what to do with myself while I waited, saw the weather tower far out and almost complete, putting its mark on the horizon, and a stomach-sour anger took me. I'm sick of that thing and it has only just arrived. My feeling anything won't make it go away.

Keys were in the house but there's a spare in the shop. Started the truck and drove south to the first crossroad. Drove west.

The tower was farther out than I expected. Seemed it got bigger the longer I drove but not any closer. That worsened the sourness in me. Forty or fifty miles out, hit a crossroad where I could see more traffic had been going—there was caked mud and dust on the pavement—so turned in that direction and soon found a dirt scratch cutting through the prairie toward the tower. From the road I could see two cranes and a job trailer and all these stacks of material, and it was all up on a small rise but when I got there, there were no men working. The site was empty. Just machines and material. Got out the truck and took a few steps toward the thing. Then I just kind of stood there. It was likely two hundred feet tall. Just four long legs and metal Xs zipping up in between. It looked like it should all lead up to something. But at the top, there was just a red glass lantern. Like a lighthouse in the prairie.

I stood there a while feeling helpless. Scooped up a rock and threw it, but the rock sailed right through, missing the legs and braces and landing in the dirt with a poof. I suppose this is what impotence feels like. They take everything away and bury it behind some church somewhere and leave you nothing but the world stretching wide all around you. But they won't even leave you that. They build a lighthouse where there is no water, just something to remind you that even this they've taken away. You can't even look upon a goddamn sunset without being reminded of some lost time that was better. It grants no mercy to us trying to forget.

I do not remember driving home. The boy and his ugly girl were fawning over the foal. They waved when they seen I was back. Somehow, seeing that made everything worse. Went into the workshop and for the first time in years, shut the door.

June 23rd, 1965

Over dinner asked the boy if he'd like to ride the fences with me and repair what needed repairing. Not just the far-side of the orchards. The whole back forty. The boundary lines and interior partitions. We could harness a mule and load the cart with new fence posts and boards. We could pack tools and food and bedrolls, take it easy and camp out when we had a mind to. Take a few days. Make an adventure out of it. I asked him if he'd like that. But he didn't say anything.

I told him the best thing to do when you see a rattlesnake is to pretend you don't see a rattlesnake. Just walk the other way. Let it be. I asked him, does that make sense?

I waited for him to answer. Then I told him: we are going to repair the fences. We will harness a mule and load the cart with provisions. We will work as a team and sleep in the fields. I didn't try to make it sound fun this time. Made it sound like the work it was. I asked him, did he understand?

The boy responded with a very slow nod. When I asked him to say it, he said he understood. There wasn't any life in his voice or in his eyes. He stared at his plate awhile then got up and left the room. He put on his record of bird songs.

He does not understand yet that a kind person can be hard sometimes and still not be a mean person. Just as a cruel person can sometimes grant favors and still not be generous. All he sees is me being firm or silent or pushing, and that makes me a bully or greedy or unfeeling. He isn't curious about the why. Or he's already made up his mind. And what he's made up is wrong. If it was just me here now, I wouldn't give a damn. I'd likely let all the horses go and get wild on their own. Or I would lead them to someplace greater than this. Take nothing else and ride north. Manitoba or Saskatchewan. What we think is big is small up there. What we call empty is full. I would lead the horses until they chose to lead themselves, tear their hooves away from me in some unending Canadian prairie. I would leave them and ride up where I could be so small that I wouldn't even exist. That would be a solution to all things.

It is for the boy that I do not do that. Instead, I do everything else. He's too much of a child to understand.

June 24ᵗʰ, 1965

I have let the issue of repairing the fence slide.

The boy's gone over to the Hautenots' for supper. He

still is not talking to me. He's taken Coyote along but it's a long pasture ride to take in the dark. I do not suspect he will be back tonight. I had hoped this time would bring us closer together. I know, it is something we both need now. A proximity not just of flesh. But I feel instead that we're driven apart. There is no question that I am to blame. He sees me as stubborn and maybe a little cold in my heart. How can I know if he's wrong? With only two of us here, there is nothing else to contrast me to, no other voice to provide context. And maybe I am different now. In our solitude, I've become something I was not before. I would not need defending if it weren't just he and I. There'd be nothing to defend. I hope in his adulthood he does not look back on me with resentment and disappointment. I would rather he hate me, as hate is close to love. But disappointment is an open gate to not caring. I do not want him to learn to not care about his father. But he probably will.

Alone, I saw no point in cooking supper. I worked on a saddle the Fensters had left me to repair. I checked in on the beetle and spider and bird. When the sun was aiming to set, I headed westward from the house, just so far as to put the orchard at my back. I wanted an unimpeded view of the grasses and far hills and the sun. The clouds spread the light around so the whole sky was hot and waxy. There was wind. There came a point when everything was red. The sun red. The prairie red. The

Missouri River which I cannot see and the faraway hills and the Bad Lands all red as a liquid and beating heart. In the weather tower, now complete, a single red light. If I looked at my hands, they'd have been red too. But I did not look at myself.

I asked if you were far away.

You said, "I am."

I asked if I was making a mistake.

You said I am.

But you would not tell me what it was.

I know there will be a time when this distance is not so great. When I am allowed to touch you again. But that time is so far away. I asked if I would get this right but already, you were gone behind the hills, and everything in the world was blue.

June 25ᵗʰ, 1965

The bird and beetle are gone.

GOLD & RUST

Something probably matters. Events or conversations, details that have shaped Cuthbert into the man he's become. His childhood, for example—his older sister like a silent guard, their mother working, their father only sometimes around—or maybe his education. Or his job, what it was and how he lost it. Perhaps the women he's known factor in. Then again, maybe not. Maybe even if everything had gone right for Cuth (times have never been that bad), he'd still feel how he feels, still be exactly what he is: a repeat suicide, a failure at living as well as at death. Maybe this is all he could ever be, the only alternative being an instance where he's never been born. Maybe this empty stretch of gravel road is the only place he was ever meant to be.

He had to step over so many sleeping bodies to get the rope down from the rafter in his living room. The hitchhiker he picked up months ago and who's dropped in unannounced now and then ever since decided that

Cuth's house—so big and so empty—would make for a great party spot. And it did. All those strangers having so much fun. Lounging in his empty rooms. Playing games in his empty lawn. Cuth came home from a day spent confronting the ocean's ceaseless glare and all these kids with their matted hair and pungent smokes welcomed him in, offered to him whatever kindness they could, as if he was a guest and not their host. He saw no point to kicking them out. This moment versus his six years: in his home, they were living more now than he ever had. He quietly watched them celebrate themselves through the night, then took down the rope with which he'd tried to hang himself twice in the past year, slipped out into the autumn dawn and drove into the undeveloped territory north of the city. Pulled off the road and into the tall grass swaying high above the roof of his car. The grass bent down by the tires will soon rise up again. His car will be hidden by blades. Leaving his keys in the ignition, Cuth steps through the grass under a pale grey sky, does not look back.

Her invitations a seduction and a threat: the ocean is nothing to blithely walk into. Cuth spent yesterday convincing her to embrace him. To let her waves dash him against the rocks. Allow her current to drag him under and out to a place where he might never be found. But as hateful as the ocean is, she alone chooses those she destroys. As he perched himself on the tip of a stone plunging steeply into the water, the waves crashed in and roared around him like lions or temples collapsing but never took him, parting always to keep him in safety's hands. The tide peaked and receded. She didn't want him. In many ways, Cuth can't fault her choice.

The clouds thinly keep the sun wound up in a gauze, and there's a constant whisper, some secret: the sound of all those stalks of grass touching and slipping together as Cuth weaves in among them. He tries to break it down, to hear not ten thousand blades but only one, just one narrow finger of grass, the individual that makes up the whole. But he cannot. He can't identify the one from the many.

The choice was binary, the time he first brought the hitchhiker into his home. He could have just as easily dumped him off somewhere in town. Instead, he offered him some floor for his bedroll. The hitchhiker dumped his stuff in the kitchen and wandered the afternoon dimness of the house, Cuth following behind, as if he was the one who needed a guide. In the room with only a typewriter and stool inside, the kid asked if Cuth wrote. In the room with only a folding chair and guitar, he asked if he played. To both, Cuth said no. "They just needed somewhere to go." Regarding the noose drooping from the living room's X of rafters—more laziness than any-thing symbolic—the kid said nothing, only pointed and tried to meet Cuth's eyes. But he owed no one an explanation. Cuth shrugged then left for the kitchen, to peel open a can and warm some beans for their supper.

Beyond the tall swishing grass runs a rocky meadow sloping up to a dense wood of maple and poplar and ash. This deep in October, everything is orange or yellow or red. And beyond the trees: a low mountain, tomb blue and severe as a wolf's tooth. Once in the summer, when the earth and air smelled hot and alive, Cuth stood in this same meadow between the tall grass and trees, having pulled his car off to the side of the road to watch a black mass of storm roll in off the mountain, wash in around him and roar and move on. It felt like some sort of sign, but in another language, full of meaning yet indicating nothing. Now he stands in roughly the same spot, the same grass at his back, the same trees and mountain looming tall before him, but if he's expecting another sign then soon he'll be disappointed. Bright leaves fall from the limbs that once bore them. That is all. Only the hopeless would mistake a falling leaf for anything but what it is. Rope coiled over his shoulder, Cuth crosses the meadow to the trees.

Last winter, on New Year's morning, he tried to drown himself by smashing a hole through a river's ice and climbing under the crystalline sheet. It didn't really work out. His body plunged into the freezing water and seized tightly into a stone. He couldn't do much more than sink as the cold became a sort of warmth, a white strobe within him as everything grey and blue faded softly away. But anyway, someone found him—a game warden, no less—and dragged him out, saved him, then took him to a diner for lunch. Cuth suspects he should have acted more grateful, but disappointment's a hard shroud to shrug off. Later that spring he went back to the river, thinking he could just dive in and be washed away. But really, it was a wimpy river. More honestly called a creek. Shallow and slow. He splashed in the muck and felt like a fool. He's never gotten used to feeling like a fool.

A gentle breeze moves everywhere around him as he walks up the slope to the trees, a cool mouth or hand nuzzling fallen leaves. The soft sounds make him think he's surrounded by animals, and when he looks around, he's surprised to see that yes, there are actual animals. Watching him. Aware. Some ten yards ahead, a rabbit swiftly nibbles at the meadow grass, and beyond that, in the dimness of the forest understory: a fox, still and watching the rabbit watch Cuth. Because it's what all people do—suicides or otherwise—Cuth pauses to watch the animals, to watch himself be watched, and in a subtle but sudden moment he becomes aware that he is surrounded. Countless rabbits move about the meadow, chewing, hopping, while in the woods a legion of foxes looks on. Rusty coats and golden eyes. Observed and observing. A fairytale or dream. Rabbits safely exposed in the light. Foxes like memories, darting in the dark. Cuth waits for the movements to dissolve, fading back into the landscape from which they emerged until he is alone again in the meadow. No rabbits. No fox. Only himself and the wind. Cuth steps in among the trees.

Once Cuth drew a bath for himself and some razorblades. It was an attempt at tradition, a classical sort of end, but he couldn't understand how the components fit together. Hot water and open veins, tiny planes of steel. Was it symbolic for making oneself clean? Or was it just a measure of comfort, a soothing bath while dying? He was stymied by his lack of understanding: the only person disallowed confusion over a suicide is the suicide himself. And anyway, the razors kept slipping through his wet fingers. He washed and went to bed instead, and later that night dreamed that he was taking a shower and while lathering his torso, noticed a tiny pink bubble on his belly. Like a small piece of strawberry gum, just to the left of his navel. In the dream, he tried to pick off the tiny pinkness, but it only grew longer, extending as a tube. The more he tried to remove it from his body, the more there was to remove. Like into sleep, slowly, he saw that what he was pulling on was coming tenderly from inside him. Yet still: he pulled. It was in this way, amid the steam and hot water, that Cuth tugged out his insides. This dream comes and goes every few months—like the hitchhiker, like his failed deaths. He's never considered it a nightmare.

The second or third time the hitchhiker showed up,

he brought with him a friend. Small and dark and somehow folded inward, as if carrying a wound close to his lungs or spleen. The friend barely spoke. The two showed up with their backpacks full of food, and whether it was stolen or foraged from trashcans, Cuth couldn't care. For three days, the two cooked and ate and cleaned and cooked in a perpetual, unsated cycle and in the evenings they'd sit—the three of them—amid the crickets and mosquitoes and the sound of the hitchhiker playing Cuth's guitar, gently strumming old Neil Young songs or Hank Williams or Townes Van Zandt. His voice wasn't much but his picking was fine. It was the sort of thing Cuth noticed only once they were gone. But after that, the hitchhiker never arrived alone.

He even bought a gun. A .357 and a box of hollow points: perfectly assured destruction. But that option overall was too messy. It didn't seem fair that someone else would have to clean up all that blood and skull and brain. The point would be totally missed.

Walking among the trees—the white peeling bark and rough plated bark, the fluttering mosaic of reds and golds—Cuth briefly forgets why he's here. The smell of earth and leaves. The cloud-diffused sun cutting through the canopy above. The quick skittering of animals dashing unseen. It's really quite a beautiful day.

Orchestrating a car accident guarantees nothing, and again: messy. The tedium of an overdose isn't even really like dying. Are you truly choosing death if you're sleeping through the best part? Or are you simply trying to escape?

Over a rocky bluff shaped like a president's forehead, amid a crown of swaybacked saplings and nodding green ferns, Cuth finds it. Tall and ancient. A maple that cannot fail him. High above is where birds likely nest. Among its roots, moles and snakes burrow. Securing the coil around his shoulder, Cuth fits his hands and feet into the bark, feels an immediate intimacy with its touch and scent as he grapples at its branches, moves up its armored body.

During last night's party, Cuth discovered the hitch-hiker upstairs in the typewriter's room, actively blowing minds. He was holding court at the room's center, a dozen or more kids sitting or standing around him, listening as he explained the basics of infinite regressions.

"This is an easy one, guys. You're crossing the street, right? A simple enough affair. Mathematically, this would be described as moving from Point A to Point B. Your path would be a line, but whatever, you're crossing a street. Of course, before you can reach Point B on the far side of the street, you have to get halfway. Right? And before you get halfway, you have to get halfway to that point, and before you get halfway to the halfway, you have to get halfway *there* and . . . " He trails off as a general giggly murmur rises and falls. "This isn't groundbreaking science, you know? If you have to reach the halfway mark between each point on the line, and there is obviously an infinite number of halves of halves of halves, then clearly it's impossible to ever move anywhere. You're always only ever trying to get halfway. And the same is true in life. In actual living. At one point we do not exist and then, somehow, we do. So there's got to be an infinite number of steps between nonexistence and personhood, too, right? We didn't just spring fully formed from the universal consciousness. There are steps to existing, and half steps, and halves of halves. So you can't possibly cross that gap between nothingness and somethingness, just as you can't possibly cross the street. Yet we do. Every day. We cross streets. We exist."

The hitchhiker's last remarks are aimed directly at Cuth, over the heads and past the bodies. Cuth sees what he's up to and sees that it's bullshit. These sorts of paradoxes only work if you do not acknowledge the difference between the infinitely large and the infinitely small. The universe is infinite in its vastness, is transfinite, impossible to cross or ever comprehend, and thus has meaning. Humans are infinitesimal, have no weight or impact, mean nothing. We are the halves, he thinks but does not say as he steps out into the hall. The universe is the line. We're each a nonevent.

This silent argument is the closest Cuth has ever come to justifying himself: if we are so close to being nothing already, why not cease the dithering and simply become nothing? He feels this logic is sound. Even still, this too is bullshit and he knows it. Mathematics can explain everything but this. For more than anything else, Cuth wants to disappear. To dissolve back into the womb of the world, leaving no trace of himself behind. Because this doesn't feel like existence. Some mistake has obviously been made, and where there should be nothing—a blankness, a breeze—he instead resides. It's unclear how long he's felt this way. Maybe forever, only more strongly now, more clearly. He hasn't had a legitimate friend in years, at least none still living. What little family he has sees no use in him: he does not disabuse them of this fact. He didn't intentionally lose his job, but he certainly did nothing to save it. For years, he's been passing through the still pool of the world with barely a ripple, accentuating his nothingness, doing his best to reclaim his lack of existence. The only thing left to confirm his insubstantiality is to finally and irrevocably disappear. And one cannot disappear if someone finds the body.

Miles from any road and twenty feet up a tree, Cuth finds the branch he wants. Thick and strong with a clear path underneath. He measures out a few arm-lengths of rope and ties it to the limb. Enough for an effective drop, one that might crush his windpipe but not so much as to break his neck: he wants to feel the slow fade of everything without breath. Easily, comfortably, he winds the familiar swoops of a new noose, fits the loop over his neck, cinches it in. This has always been his favorite, the hanging, though it too never works. The first time, on a chair under the rafters, his phone began to ring. Who wants to die to a chorus of fake bells? He answered the call, spoke with a woman and then later, had sex. Months after that, the mail carrier came knocking to deliver a package to the wrong address. That time, Cuth had already tipped himself off the chair, was swinging peacefully but then struggling to get free, to tell this stranger to fuck off. It was nauseating, his shift from calm to panic, acceptance to anger. Like hustling along the highway and suddenly dropping into reverse. He's still not sure how he made it down.

Overhead, a flock of southbound geese passes, honking and calling ceaselessly to one another, a perpetual song of *I'm here, I'm right here* that will not end until they've gotten to where they're going. On his limb, ready to fall, Cuth listens to them come and go, and as their calls diminish, he becomes aware of a new sound. Coughing and insistent and not too far away. If not human then a byproduct thereof. Some kind of engine. Two-stroke. A machine. Holding the noose like some bleak rosary, Cuth mutters the first words he's said all day:

"You gotta be fucking kidding me."

Dry and croaking, by disuse or constriction. He unties the rope and slides back down the tree.

It never occurs to Cuth that the hitchhiker might have a reason for wanting him not to die. To Cuth, it's merely an obstacle. A knock at the door. A hand fishing him from the water. There's always a body blocking his path.

At first he thinks he's getting further away, to some more isolated stretch of woods—closer to the mountain maybe—but the sound doesn't seem to be retreating at all, seems to actually be getting closer. Gradually, he realizes that he's seeking it out. He wants to know what's keeping him alive this time.

Lindsay was the woman who called when he first tried to hang himself, the first time he tried to die. It unnerves him how the question will rise up out of his sleep in those early dark hours: what would have happened if the two of them had worked out? The fact that this question resides in him—in his unconscious, no less—fills him with doubt about everything he's done. So he does not acknowledge the question. There are some rabbit holes that even he will not gaze down.

He knows the clearing isn't natural because all the trees are lying in the same direction. All but one. The one that's fallen wrong is huge and mighty looking, and the man underneath it was maybe mighty once too but now looks pale and surprised. But how surprised can a dead person be? The dead are never surprised. Beside the man and the tree that killed him lies the chainsaw that killed them both, idling and nestled in the blanketing gold leaves like a purring, satiated cat. The whole scene is almost peaceful.

Cuth stands stilly amid this for a while. Then he kneels.

The man was probably in his fifties. Blonde going to silver. Flannel pants and green plaid shirt. A few feet away, his orange helmet lies where it fell and rolled from his head. A thin gloss of blood on his lips. He probably knew exactly what he was doing out here, right up until the moment when he didn't. It's funny, Cuth thinks, how some mistakes can't possibly be learned from. On the man's left hand—the hand not hidden beneath the fallen tree—Cuth finds a wedding band, dulled by years yet gleaming still. He wonders if there's a wife somewhere waiting for this man. He wonders if she's maybe long gone, this ring and his memories being all she left him with. Or maybe he left her and his fingers swelled and the ring would never come off: cursed by the jilted. Or maybe theirs is a marriage of strength and silence. Or maybe his wife, too, has died. So many shades of grey in between. Like the dead man's skin. Like the sky. How can there be no peace in something so peaceful, so passive, so still? Cuth closes the man's eyes, but the mouth will not close. Locked in a shocked and open O. Which strikes him as the most horrible part of all.

Sometimes, Cuth goes to the junkyard to watch the crusher crush the lost and abandoned cars. Broken windows and rusted fenders. Waste made small but nevertheless waste. Among the leaves of the forest, the wind nestles and moves. Somewhere, a fox watches a shadow. Somewhere, a shadow watches itself. Reaching over, Cuth clicks off the saw. Is locked in the silence until the silence is unlocked. Then he turns on his cell phone and calls for someone to help.

ACKNOWLEDGMENTS

Nearly half of the stories in this collection were written during fellowships with the Hewnoaks Artists Colony and the I-Park Foundation, each of whose haunted geographies have left indelible imprints, not only on the work drafted in one lonesome cabin or another, but on everything I've written since. In similar fashion, the past and present transactors at SPACE—by both repeatedly championing my work and allowing generous use of their galleries as both performative and generative venues—are responsible for more of my creative output than they can possibly know. And too, without the cheerleading, promotion, and all-round support of the Maine Writers & Publishers Alliance, I would unquestionably have one less blue balloon to bandy proudly about. For all the above, I am humbled in gratitude.

Without the journals and small presses who first published these stories—some of whose acceptance letters arrived on the days I felt most convinced of my perpetual failings—I likely would never have completed this book. I am forever indebted to the editors of the *Stoneslide Corrective*, *Slice*, *Glimmer Train*, the *Adirondack Review*, *Camera Obscura*, the *Lascaux Review*, the *Maine Review*, *Per Contra*, the *Midwest Prairie Review*, the *Lindenwood Review*, the *Island Journal*, the *Cortland Review*, and *Portland Monthly*, as well as to Sam Gould at Beyond Repair and Bill Henderson at Pushcart Press for providing first (and sometimes second) audiences to these stories.

In the nine years over which *Blue of the World* was written, several early readers were instrumental in helping transform my half-formed ideas into coherent narratives— most especially Jacob Cholak, Mandy Moorish, Andrew Lyman, Eric Schwan, Michael Dix Thomas, Derek Kimball, Scott Sell, Patrick Kiley, Anne Danae, Justin Woollard, Ben Trickey, Megan Grumbling, Jenna Crowder, Carmiel Banasky, and Mark Priola—even if (especially when) I took the exact opposite route recommended. Thank you for your insights, and more importantly, thank you for your patience.

A very specific thank you to Cat Bates for the magnitude of trust placed in me and the intimacy that comes with that, as well as for continuing to collaborate with me on increasingly unusual narrative multimedia.

And finally, greatest thanks to Genevieve Johnson, for making possible, for sustaining, for breathing vitality into this bizarro life we've chosen together.

ABOUT THE AUTHOR

DOUGLAS W. MILLIKEN is the author of two novels—*To Sleep as Animals* and *Our Shadows' Voice*—as well as several chapbooks and collaborative multimedia projects, including *In the Mines* with the musician Scott Sell and *Monolith* with the metal smith Cat Bates. He has won numerous awards for his short stories, including *Glimmer Train*'s "Family Matters" contest, a Maine Literary Award for Short Fiction, a Pushcart Prize, and the *Stoneslide Corrective*'s annual Short Story Contest. He is exhausted by the mouse chorus of souls following his heartless kitten through the understory. He lives with his contra-wife in Saco, Maine.

Also by Douglas W. Milliken

White Horses
To Sleep as Animals
Brand New Moon
Cream River
One Thousand Owls Behind Your Chest
Monolith (with Cat Bates)
The Opposite of Prayer
In the Mines (with Scott Sell)
Our Shadows' Voice

www.ingramcontent.com/pod-product-compliance
Lightning Source LLC
Chambersburg PA
CBHW050301110726
47898CB00007B/2492